Minstrels' Prize

Book III

of

The Minstrels' Tale Mystery

by

Nance Bulow Morgan

Dreamer Books

Marston, NC

Dreamer Books, Marston, NC
www.dreamerdesigns.net

ISBN: 978-0-9915625-2-7
Library of Congress Control Number: 201590411

Nance Bulow-Morgan

Nance Bulow-Morgan and the Dreamer Books Logo are trademarks belonging to Nance Bulow-Morgan

CREATED AND PRINTED IN THE UNITED STATES OF AMERICA

·~·Dedication·~·

To those of you who hold on tight even in the face of doubt
and,
for The Great All In All, The One God.

I hope that my ordinary act might have extraordinary results.

·~·Acknowledgments·~·

I'd like to give a very special thanks to Aaron Jindrich. When I was struggling through the logistics of the first book she suggested that I change a plot tool from books to music. It was a stroke of genius that she graciously gifted to me. Thanks so much Aaron, you saved the day!

·~·Foreword·~·

When Andreas and I chased a murderer across the sea our adventure became a quest to save seven kings and seven kingdoms. We were forced to separate to advance our end. Those were dire times and they caused us to admit our relationship was more than just friendship. We re-examined ourselves, our purpose, and our relationship.

Our missions were successful even though two kings were lost to intrigue. The countries survived and became unified. As thanks we were gifted one of the dispossessed kingdoms. We saw it as a chance to build a life together and we accepted. We left our Kingdom of Breen in good hands until we could return. We were married in Mareese and celebrated our nuptial quietly while winter passed outside.

During that time Andreas finished deciphering the ledger we obtained while solving another murder; that of the great procurer, Eindal. In that ledger is a list of powerful people, places, and things. One item caught our eyes; an item made for good; stolen into evil hands. Our moral leanings could not let such a thing stand.

Our reputation as minstrels is well known, and had even elevated to the status of bard, but it is our skill as elementalist and warrior that kept us in a game of cat and mouse with Lord Devil and his union of evil.

This is a story of casting off what we believed to be truth. It is a story of overcoming our doubts, beating down our demons, and accepting new truths; no matter how incredible they are.

I will begin this tale as we contemplate the contents of Eindal's ledger... .

·~·Table of Contents·~·

·~·Chapter One·~·

The fresh spring breeze rushed softly through our window and played with the corners of the pages laid in my lap. Andreas sat beside me on the floor at the foot of our bed. Our heads leaned into each other as we looked over the transcribed ledger of Eindal, the purveyor of rare items.

Eindal was the victim in our first murder case. His death propelled us into a great undertaking that involved many people and realms. Eindal was attempting to deliver news that he had found the means to stop the unlocking of Hell gates. He was killed before revealing it. Our investigation served his ends and those gates that had been opened were locked again. We saved the ledger and Andreas spent a good deal of time repairing and deciphering it from the ancient arcane language.

We spent that great long afternoon reveling in the comfort of our marriage. We sipped brandy and read the transcription of Eindal's procurement ledger. There were many interesting people and places mentioned among the items within the entries, but the most fantastic entry was an orb called God's Iris, or God's Eye as Andreas had come to call it.

Eindal's notes transcribed into our own language produced a description that was hard to believe, but believe we did. After all; it was Eindal who had at first led us to the three scrolls that re-locked the gates of Hell.

I read; The Eye was a star formed when God's own hands compressed it until it exploded. He continued to compress it even as it exploded again and again between the strength of his hands. The elements within his grasp became an azure blue crystal with the strength of raw tungsten. Eindal's various theories about the orb's purpose were like the imaginings of a child. He settled on the theory that God instilled it with the ability to travel through the cosmos, and that whoever was in possession of The Eye could hear God and speak with Him.

The cosmos was a place so vast that my mind had trouble comprehending it. It was Heaven and Hell, here and away, unknown places within a universe we had not known, existed.

I doubted the existence of one all powerful god very much. He had never come to me, even in my most desperate prayers. Most of my life had been wrought with dangers and temptations of evil. Perhaps the part of me that was demon spawn called that down on me. I wanted to believe there was a way to neutralize the demons and devils of shadows. I wanted to believe in minions of light. Sadly, Andreas's transcription made no mention of such beings.

I read on. Eindal had based his information about The Eye on a conversation with a contact he made in a city called Koman. Father Gan had once spoken of demonic influences throughout the population there. Koman was a place known to breed people of evil intentions. Eindal's contact answered to the name Jest. Such a name seemed obviously chosen to protect his true identity, but who gave it, Eindal or the man? Whoever Jest was we were interested in talking to him.

Koman was situated on a cold and jagged coast in the rough seas beyond Thunderhead and Winter Top, on an island, also called Koman. Mountains encroached on the city from three sides. Somewhere in those mountains was an asylum. In our quest for the three scrolls we learned that the asylum hid one of three points of entrance to three of the gates that led to the nine hells. We had some idea what laid beyond those gates. We had been to Hell by a different gate.

Eindal's notes revealed that his contact had seen a battle between the forces of good and evil in the mountains surrounding the asylum. Evil had won that day. In the spoils of the battle lay an orb that shone with a most beautiful blue aura. Devil's soldiers feared to touch it and carefully wrapped it in cloth and returned to the asylum with it.

Andreas believed, and I agreed that if God's Iris was on Earth and in the hands of someone in Koman, or worse in Hell itself; it would be a very bad thing for Earth. If all of this was true, and it likely was, based on Eindal's renown as a procurer of rare and mystical items, then we had our work cut out for us. What evil could be brought from other worlds? What havoc could evil bring to those worlds? What fight between Heaven and Hell could cause God to let so powerful a thing out of his control? Was it possible that someone of great evil had possession of it still? Could they have somehow harmed an all powerful God?! Was that why so many thought ill of Him, or like me, doubted His existence?

We were certain that we had to retrieve the item. What we would do with it then we did not know, but it did not sit well with us to know that such a thing lay in the hands of evil.

Our cozy day took on a morbid atmosphere. We discussed the quest. It would require sailing over open water once again. I never did well with that, but with green root under my tongue I could bear it. In the scope of what we were about to undertake, that was a minor thing. The thought of piercing the barrier between Earth and Hell drew us both into dark and reflective moods. To do that would risk all that we had fought for to lock the gates. Our peaceful existence was about to be turned upside down. Our actions could jeopardize the peace of the whole world.

I wished Andreas had never showed me that damned ledger, yet, I felt we owed it to Eindal. He lost his life attempting to bring news of the musical scores that were the keys to locking the gates of Hell forever. If we had been able to talk to him then, perhaps he would have told us of The Eye. It could have become part of that mission. We put our faith in Eindal's information and proposed to do what we could.

"How do you think Eindal gets his information about the items in his ledger?" I asked Andreas as he stretched in our bed.

"Rumors, old wives tales. I'm sure he had to weed that all out until he could follow a solid line of legend. Legends seem most likely."

"The Legend of The Eye," I said in my best dramatic tone. "That seems very unlikely. Don't you think we would have heard of it before if it had been legend?"

"Theology then? Eindal was surrounded by a consortium of great thinkers many of whom were theologians."

"Perhaps."

"Do you still doubt that there is a god; after all that you have seen?"

"I have not seen a god in my life."

"Do you need to see Him to believe?"

"I need at least to feel Him, to have some sign of His existence."

"Perhaps you haven't been paying attention."

"So you believe that some god has had a hand in my life? Hard to put trust in a god who would abandon women and children."

"Do you never wonder how it is that we are still alive? Do you never wonder that I came into your life just as you needed me the most?"

I laughed aloud, "Next you will say that you are my guardian angel."

"Guardian mortal, perhaps. Divine intervention maybe; fate, or destiny."

"I need to get you out of Mareese. You are beginning to sound like one of those mystics."

"I am just saying that I am open to all things. You always look to the dark side of things. Perhaps I was sent to keep you toward the light."

"I blame the dark on my father, but you are right that things would be darker without you."

He kissed my forehead. "So I am the light of your life then," he said and smiled that heart melting smile of his.

"Yes, Love."

"Good, and don't you forget it."

"You won't let me."

"How do you know that your father is not a god?"

"Careful now. Some might call that blasphemy."

"Not the One God of All, but a god. A god of darkness and evil things I'll grant; from some realm we don't understand. Still what do we know about it? Even the God of All recognizes a heavenly host. Could there then be a Hellish host?"

"Sometimes I hate it when you think."

"Me too, but you can't deny that from what we have witnessed it is possible."

I moved closer to him and he but his arms around me. I found comfort there from the dark mood that had consumed our day. We stayed awhile lost in the quiet and our thoughts. Until Andreas broke the silence.

"I'm hungry. What do we have?" He jumped up and crossed to the pantry of the small apartment. His body was lithe and graceful as he moved. He was shirtless. Scars of old battles bulged in every area of his body, but still he was beautiful.

He was such an enigma to me. He could be so wicked when faced with adversity, yet so kind when faced with the turmoil of others. His mind and wit were sharp; they always prevailed. When he dropped a faux-pas in court he always charmed his way back into good graces. When faced with a suspected adversary I had learned that it was better to let him do the talking; most of the time. I was too direct and could insult without regret, or sometimes without knowing. Andreas though, was subtle and people liked him right off. I was guarded and that was often mistaken for arrogance.

I watched as he built a small fire in the hearth. When it was going well I went and gathered ingredients to make pork soup. As I cut the vegetables into the water in a kettle over the fire I watched him dress. I was very lucky to have him in my life.

I wondered why we did not just settle down. We had status as minstrels and made enough to survive by playing at Diony's court, at fairs, local pubs, or just along the streets with a hat out for contributions. We had a good deal of wealth safe in the governor's treasury. "Why do we not just settle down, Andy? We said once that we would."

"We did, didn't we? Is it want you want? We have seen much in our lives Perhaps we should bring this ledger to Diony. She can find someone else to save the world. No one can say we haven't done our part."

It was what I wanted, to have a stable life but the problem before us prevailed. "I don't see how we can now. We cannot let God's Eye remain in the hands of devils. We have the experience. Diony will just ask us to go."

"You are right, of course. There is much of the world we have *not* seen. We will just have to take the good with the bad. Perhaps we will even see a god."

"Sure."

"You cannot fool me, Sade. You want to know."

"Yes, you are right as always. Do we have to find out by going into Hell to do it? I desire a god of good, yet we go and seek one in the domain of evil."

He smiled. "Perhaps it is what we must bear. Perhaps we are even chosen for it."

"All I know is that we must go. I could not bear it if my reluctance kept God's property in the clutches of evil to be perverted into something heinous."

"That a girl, never quit believing."

"I'd have to start first."

"Oh come on. You aren't fooling me. You pray over every death after a battle."

"Just in case; because I've been to Hell. I don't want to send anyone else there if I can prevent it with a prayer of passage."

We went quiet for a time. I spooned the soup into bowls and we ate while lost in thought.

I broke the silence as we cleaned up the meal. "So, are we really going to do this then?" I asked.

"You yourself said you couldn't bear it if reluctance kept the Iris in Hell's clutches."

"I would have to go and say that aloud. It's true; though I dread the whole idea."

"You aren't alone in that."

"So what do we do first; notify next of kin?" I asked.

"I was thinking maybe we should just tell everyone we were taking a long awaited honeymoon trip."

"To Koman? No one will believe that."

"We'll have to lie about that part," he said.

"I'll leave that to you. You are so good at it."

"Comes from years of keeping my talents hidden from my family."

"Will you notify them?"

"Actually, I was thinking it might be time they meet my bride—that is until this came up. For now I will just write a letter. They will be shocked. I haven't contacted them since my father cast me out. It will give my mother comfort to know that I won't die alone."

"We still have Breen to worry about," I offered. "I suppose we must see to our obligations to mortal men, but I hate to take the time."

"We have become stewards of the people there. It is a sacred pact to be a landlord. We can't wait much longer. We cannot know how long this quest will take. The time of gods seem to move much slower and more deliberately than that of mortal men."

"Okay, we will take possession of Breen. As soon as things are settled there we will sail for Koman."

We made our plans and went out into the city to make arrangements for them. We went to see Governor Diony Vin Heile first, to make arrangements for my Mam and our foster, Mya's safety until we could return and bring them to Breen. We made no hint of our quest, proceeding only as newly pledged rulers of a dispossessed kingdom.

Andreas began to tell them we were leaving, when Diony gave an audible gasp of dismay.

"My minstrels, my friends, I knew it was coming, but how can you leave us?"

"Life keeps turning, m'lady. For us it turns to Breen. We will be allies to you there and help to settle the details of the treaty. When do the Ahngesian dignitaries arrive?"

"Not until summer. Will you be back then? It would be right for you to be present. You have a stake in this treaty now too."

I said. "That, in part is why we have come to you today. We need a swift ship with a keen crew who can take us where we want to go. In fact we would like someone who is willing to stay in our employ. A king and queen of a seaside kingdom should have a suitable ship, captain, and crew. We thought that you could recommend someone who would fit the bill and be trustworthy."

Diony's man, Brynal had been a sailor for most of his young life. We were confident he would be able to recommend a suitable ship, captain, and crew. Our friends hashed out possible candidates and settled on one that pleased them both.

"Nights, he is the captain for you," Brynal declared. "They call him Nights because he is as dark as a moonless night. He laughs at the name and will introduce himself that way. His real name is Lio Nihoc. He is one of the best captains on the water; smart and daring, but also wise. He has been all around the world and has a sense of adventure, a quality

I'm sure will make you all fast friends. He is getting older though and is looking to get out of the trade markets. What you offer him would be like a pleasure cruise—a happy retirement. Maybe he will settle down at last.

"We will talk to him. What is the name of his boat?"

"Ship, don't ever call it a boat. He finds that insulting. He named it Night's Angel."

Andreas and I were amazed. So much of our private plans had included talk about deities and spirits

I looked away to hide my surprise, while Andreas managed to say; "Good name."

Governor Diony changed the subject then and asked after my mother's well being, "Has your Mam come to terms with leaving her shop?"

"I believe she is actually looking forward to the change now. She has been working with the new apothecary for several weeks and they have become friends. She speaks highly of him. Mam has so much knowledge and this young man is a good student. His wife is an artist. They have a child on the way. Mareese will be a good home for them. Mam is happy to turn her shop over to someone who will take care of it for a long time. She is also thrilled about being the only apothecary on all of Ahnges.

"I am not convinced that moving her to Breen now makes sense. With Gebha, the assassin still out there I think she will be safer here, where people we know and trust can watch out for her. When we have secured Breen and we are comfortable with the changes there then we will come for her. We hope that will be in the summer during the treaty talks."

We stayed a couple of hours enjoying the company of good friends and seeing to arrangements for Mam and Mya. When all was set we were confident that Mam would be pleased and that Diony would see to her safety.

9

Mam and Mya would move into the east tower and act as apothecary to Diony and her house. This would give them both experience living in the daily routines of a noble leader's home and life. Mam would move her shop to the tower, and the new apothecary would then move in to the old shop. That kept Mam and Mya safe, and gave the new and old apothecary a comfortable transition that would still allow them to interact if needed.

When we left the manor we said our goodbyes. Mareese had given us peace and good friends. No matter what we had said to Diony and Brynal, we did not know if we would ever return. We struggled to keep our emotions in check. If we were fortunate enough to return from Hell again we would still be far away tending our interests in Breen.

Perhaps we had been greedy to accept the offer of the city of Breen as our own. We discussed the possibility on our way to the wharf to look up Captain Night's ship. In the end we had done nothing wrong. We had aided the people of Ahnges and they had offered us Breen as reward. It was our right to take it. That reasoning did nothing to calm the feeling of loss that was already in our hearts.

We found the Night's Angel in a far slip and called out to those aboard. "Hello on the Night's Angel."

"Ahoy lubber, who goes there?"

"It is Andreas and Saeede. We have come with a business proposition for you?"

Nights pulled himself up the ladder from the berth deck. He was so dark skinned that his form seemed like a phantom as he moved toward the ship rail in the dark of night to look down on us. He was a massive man. Easily as tall as Andreas but twice as broad and all muscle. His head was bald, but his beard was long and braided while his mustache was tightly trimmed.

When he saw us he gave us a great warm smile. "The great minstrels of Mareese. What business proposition do you have for a lowly sailor such as I?"

"You are not so lowly as you think," Andreas said. "You come recommended by the governor's house."

"Oh, I am honored to have that recognition. Tell me then, what I have been recommended for?"

"Our conversation is of a delicate nature. I would like to not have to shout it all about here on the wharf. Can we come aboard?"

He lowered his voice then and motioned us up as he slid the plank out for us. "Oh, I see. Off on another of your great adventures then, aye?"

We nodded an affirmative response.

"Come on up. We can go to my quarters. My crew has all gone ashore, so we will be alone."

We followed him down and laid out an itinerary for him. We would leave Mareese for Nagrom. Once there he would accompany us while we took possession of Breen. Once that was done we would rejoin the ship and crew to sail on to Koman where he would wait until we finished our business there. Then back to Mareese for the summer treaty negotiations. After that back again to Breen, where we hoped to dock at a newly constructed pier. At that time we would move him and his crew into proper housing in Breen.

Nights was excited about the whole business. A lay over in Koman gave him pause, but he quickly shrugged it off and announced that he would wait for us off shore. We would have to signal the ship to have them send a dinghy to retrieve us.

Nights gave us a tour of the ship, and we were well pleased with the arrangements. The negotiated agreement was equitable for both parties.

He had a cargo he would have to sell off, but we considered him our captain from that moment on. He assured us of his men's loyalty and we set a date to sail two days out. Andreas paid him a year's wages for him and his men and we left to tell Mam of the preparations for her while we were away.

She did not take kindly to our rearranging her life without her input, but she had to admit that we had thought of everything. She and Mya were both disappointed that we would not be moving them to Breen on this trip. Mam accused us of being selfish, but we assured her we would see to it that their places were made ready for the time when we would all go to settle down together.

·~·Chapter Two·~·

The morning of our departure broke warm and breezy. Andreas and I were anxious, but we went about as casually as we could manage and introduced ourselves to the crew as they took us out to sea.

Mam had concocted a new formula to battle my seasickness and I was anxious to test its worth. I went to stand in the prow and took on the stance I had seen Andreas take so many times when we had sailed before. The feel of the wind against my face was a triumph. Joy came up in me and I threw wide my arms, tossed back my head and laughed. The wind played through my fingers and I felt like a bird in flight. I had often been jealous of Andreas as he stood reveling in the sensation of flight across the waters. I would not have to be jealous again. I blessed my mother for the gift she had given me. She did not know how great a gift it was.

"Find your wings, Angel?" I heard Andreas ask as he came to put his arms around me.

"It feels like that to me now. I used to hate that you could feel this and I could not. My mother's brew works perfectly! This is awesome!"

"Can I tear you away? I have something equally awesome to show you."

"I don't know what that could be, but I'm curious."

He took me to where several sailors were pointing at the water, laughing, and calling out in merriment. As we came to the rail I saw a school of large black and white fish. They were about twelve fotmal in length. They jumped in and out of the water, following along with us, just along our starboard side.

"You have always been so taken with the sea sickness that you've missed this before. See how the pure white center and sides of their bodies look like wings? That and the legends about them saving drowning sailors have gotten them named Angelimare. In the ancient tongue it means angel of the sea." Andreas told me this and I turned to meet his eyes.

"Yes," he said, "Angels seem to be coming at us from all sides, a synchronous situation. Everything happening seems to be connected."

"It is an odd series of coincidence that's all," I said as a way of dismissing what I felt but denied—synchronous.

It was enough to start me questioning my beliefs. Perhaps God was greeting us; giving us welcome to a mission he had patiently waited for us to take up. I watched the Angelimare and asked one of the crew how often this sort of thing happened.

"They like to play in the wake of swift ships. They stay mostly to the southern waters so it is not uncommon, but usually it is two or three. Here we have seven. That is the biggest flock I've ever seen. We sailors are a superstitious bunch. A sea angel at the start of a voyage is good luck. We must have very good luck ahead to have such a big flock to escort us."

"Flock?"

"Well they are angels and angels fly. Flock seems appropriate."

"Yes, so it does."

We spent the entire day along that rail watching and laughing and wondering at the great creatures that they were. The Angelimare were with us even as we turned north toward the southern coast of Ahnges. Often they would chirp and dance on their tails through the water. They made the most eerie, yet beautiful sounds as they chattered. They seemed to have something to say. I only wish I could have known what that was. As the suns set, the wind died, and as suddenly, as if called home the Angelimare turned as one, dove into the sea, and swam away.

The cook came to the deck and banged a wooden spoon against the deck bell to call us to dinner. We ate, then went to our cabin to gather a few instruments, to take up on deck and play for the crew. The ship moved through the water propelled more by current than wind, but we were still on our heading and the quiet seas allowed us a good audience.

We played well into morning until the spotter called out, "Land!" We were approaching Nagrom. Captain Nights guided us into a line of ships waiting to enter along one of the wharf bridges that spanned out from the shore into the sea. At the end of each of these two bridges was a harbor master's hut. We would dock there long enough to pay the dock fee and be assigned a dock.

When our turn came Captain Nights called his orders and we slid in neatly. Nights went alone to the wharf master and returned quickly with our dock assignment. He called his orders again but his men were always just ahead of him and we docked with haste and ease.

Captain Nights would accompany us to Breen to advise us about the building of a pier for his ship and a fisherman's wharf. We wanted to encourage trade with the coastal cities of Ahnges as well as Dinar, Bouthil, and Mareese. We would stop to visit with King Frahn and introduce him to our captain. Nights was happy to visit what would soon become his home.

Nights paid his men for the time that we would be laid over. His first mate was left in charge. Our horses were unloaded and we waited on the dock for Nights to complete his business.

In town we would arrange a wagon to be sent for the things going to Breen. When that wagon was loaded and delivered to Frahn's castle in our name the men were free to go into town. We did not know when we would be returning, but Nights predicted he would be back in a fortnight. He wanted to keep his crew in line and his ship at the ready.

We walked to town. Andreas and I flanked Nights and led our mounts. Grey Daria and Dark Corydon were mountain bred mounts and gifts from Kapit of Behlanna. They were sturdy and swift. We had spent many pleasant rides and hunts with them in the lands south of Mareese. There was an intelligence about them that made them more like companions than ordinary mounts.

At the stable we saw Old Sam in the yard. We waved and he came to meet us.

"Well, well. If it ain't the conquering heroes. Bless me, it is an honor to see you again."

"We are just ordinary people in extra ordinary times, Sam," Andreas said.

"It is nice to be remembered though," I added.

"Oh, you are to be sure. Things haven't been quiet the same. Peoples is, well, cheery. We get goods in from all the kingdoms now. Peoples isn't afraid to travel."

"Have you come then to take your place at Breen?"

"We have, but we want first to pay our respects to Frahn. We have need of a wagon and two good horses to move a household of goods and equipment. Our ship is in dock eight. Can you set us up?"

"That sounds like an awful lot are you sure you won't need two wagons?"

"My crew is good at packing a lot into a small area. Send your biggest wagon with a canvas and rope. They will get it done," Nights said.

We paid Sam in full for a round trip with the wagon. He noted it in his ledger and we trusted him to deliver the loaded wagon to us at Frahn's stronghold. Nights would return the wagon when he returned to his ship.

We led Daria and Corydon up to the first gate of Frahn's castle with Captain Nights beside us. The men there recognized us and greeted us as they opened for us to pass. A squire went ahead to announce us at the castle house. We walked through the outer courtyard as word of our arrival spread and the people who lived within came to greet us.

As we passed through the second gate into the castle yard we saw Frahn walk out onto the porch with his queen, Sion. We were warmly welcomed and gathered into the house almost before we could know it. Sion was a gracious hostess in this peaceful time and Frahn was much pleased with her.

"So you have come at last to take up in Breen," Frahn stated.

We did not want Frahn to know too soon about our intentions so Andreas began carefully. "We have come to tend to business there and see to comforts for Mam and Mya. They will join us later. After the treaty conference in Mareese is settled we will be in Breen and make our lives there. I warn you though, we intend to support the fishermen with a proper wharf, and from there expand to bring ships in directly to a small port. Captain Nights is coming along to advise us on that matter, then he will return here to his ship until we are ready to sail again."

"The competition is welcome, it will help us all to prosper. I am glad of it. What dock are you at Nights? I will see that your fees are waived."

"We are the Night's Angel at dock eight, thank you." Nights said.

"When do you leave for Breen?" Sion asked.

"Today, but we could not come through Nagrom without stopping to say hello. We are only waiting for our things to be off loaded from the ship and delivered to us here so that we might continue on our way."

"I am sorry that you cannot stay longer. I will at least see that a meal is packed for your travel."

"Thank you," I said.

"Will you need Pinkert to stay on there while you adjust?" Frahn asked Andreas.

"We were reluctant to ask, but if you could spare him it might be best." Andreas said.

"If he is amendable to it I see no problem. We write each other often. He is as well able to record the events of recent history from there as he could from here.

"Your people are anxious to have you in place. They were not allowed to give you proper fanfare. Your reputation makes them feel important."

"Not too important, I hope. That type of thing can breed conflict. We will learn what they need as quickly as we can. We have some funds set aside, but we must settle on a fair tax to keep the city well and safe for the future. Once we have taken measures to see that improvements are underway we have made plans for a honeymoon."

"Honeymoon?!" Sion gushed. "Surely you must stay and let us celebrate with you." She came and hugged us both. Frahn clasped Andreas on the shoulder in that brotherly way that men have.

"No we have kept the people of Breen waiting too long already. Spring is here. Travel is good. We must show them that we care." I said.

"Surely, one more day won't make that much of a difference," Sion argued.

"There will be a celebration at Breen. After all of our business is completed we will have many more reasons to celebrate. You will be our honored quests then," Andreas said. "We will go and return for good as soon as the treaty is signed. Captain Nights will see to our safe and swift passage."

"If that is what you think is best." Frahn said.

"We do," we said together.

We talked business a while longer, asking about and learning from Frahn's experiences. His teaching and our time with Diony would be useful in getting our little city in order. When our wagon was delivered neatly packed under a fully stretched canvas we said our farewells.

It was late morning when we left. Nights drove the wagon while Andreas and I rode ahead. The wagon was heavy and our way was slow. Nightfall was still early in the spring season. We pushed on into the long hours of night. Our way was lit by a lantern hung from a front sidewall beam of the wagon. Our goal was the hostel house. When we arrived it was full. We were reminded of Old Sam's declaration that people were no longer afraid to travel.

We made camp just off the road across from the hostel and took turns at watch. In the lantern light we discovered that the crew had thought-fully arranged what we needed to make camp more comfortable at the back of the wagon. Blankets rolled out beneath the wagon were our beds. In the morning we made a small fire and ate bacon and potatoes for breakfast.

In pursuit of Ambassador Esporanza's killer Andreas and I had made the trip from Nagrom to Breen in two full days. It was a wild ride then. With a heavily laden wagon we had at least two more days on the road and hoped to make Breen late on the third day. We broke camp, re-packed the wagon, then with the canvas tied down again we started out.

The time we spent together was pleasurable. Captain Nights was comfortable and warm in our company. He allowed us to call him Lio which he made certain to tell us was not an honor he gave to everyone. Lio was a humorous man and had a gift for story telling. Each night in camp we would trade stories or songs for one of his tales of the high seas. I was pleased that he had come to be our captain. Sailing with him was going to be a pleasure.

We arrived in Breen late in the evening of the third day out. The gates were closed, and the guards there did not recognize us. We were allowed to enter with an escort until someone could wake Pinkert to vouch for us. It was an odd homecoming. All the shops were closed and the houses were dark. The guards at the gate did not know us, and yet we had been the leaders of a coup that took down their pretender king.

Their king had been a fool to another king. That king conspired to bring all the kings of Ahnges down, so that he might take it all for his own.

We huddled together just inside the gate for a long time until Pinkert came at last to greet us and take us home.

·~·Chapter Three·~·

We moved into the suite of rooms that had once belonged to King Harald and his niece, the assassin, Lily-Gebha. We took Lily's old room and left Harald's bigger room for Mam. Mya's room was across the hall from the suite. Nights took a room down that hall near Pinkert.

A secret passageway in our room was compliments of Lily. It led from the back of the fireplace to an exit over the ocean inlet between the city of Breen and the fortress. It would remain a secret even from Mam and Mya. If we could not make it more secure we would block it. We could not leave Lily with a way in.

We were exhausted from our travels and slept in late the next morning. The sounds of household activity filtered up to us and urged us from our slumber. Even after waking we lingered in bed, content in the intimacy.

"You feel it too, don't you?" I asked Andreas.

"What's that?"

"Once we rise from this bed and go out of this room we will be acknowledged. We will be the King and Queen of Breen."

"And my father thought I wouldn't amount to anything."

I sat up and hugged my legs to my chest. "I don't think I am ready for this," I said and rested my chin on my knees. "I can barely keep my own life in order."

"You will be a great queen, because I am going to be a great king!"

"You hide behind bravado. I know you feel the doubt and the regret."

"Do you have regret?"

"We are giving up our lives for this. We have to lie to go in search of God's Iris. What if another opportunity presents itself? Will we lie each time, or will we pass up that which makes us feel alive—adventure?

"You make me feel alive. I need none of adventure, or this, if you are beside me. We can give it all back if you are unhappy."

I fell back into his arms and we made love.

When we were ready at last to face our new life we bathed together, then dressed plainly, but in clothes suitable to our new station. We walked the inner corridor to the stairs we had defended the night of the coup. We didn't really know our way around the place. Only those few places we had been during the coup were familiar. We wandered about and ran into Nights doing the same. We went together and found our way through the inner garden and eventually made our way to the kitchen.

Pinkert sat at a table chatting with a few of the staff over the morning meal. He stood and bowed when we came in. That act alerted the rest of the crew to who we were and a murmur of voices filled the room as they bowed too.

"Now enough of that Pinkert. We don't want people fawning all around us. Common courtesies will suffice," I said.

"But you are nobles now—royalty."

"Royalty? Royalty, royalty. No matter how I say it, it just feels wrong. I was just getting comfortable with nobility."

"Well you are King and Queen now. You must accept certain protocols. They will be expected in the courts of, and as courtesy to, other kings. You cannot allow your house to fall aside of these things."

"If it must be so then we will not breech protocol, but I doubt I will ever become accustomed to it," I said.

We took seats with Pinkert, across from the staff members.

Nia, the wife of Simo the Blacksmith, knew us. She moved through the gathered kitchen workers with our meal and placed it before us with a broad smile, but she said nothing and bowed as she retreated to a place at the front of the gathering.

I leaned over to Pinkert and asked, "Should we say something; make introductions?"

"I have arranged for you to meet all of the staff at once, but you can do as you please."

I stood, tugging at Andreas's sleeve and he joined me. "You all seem anxious to meet us and so I will make proper introductions. I am Saeede," I hesitated nearly choking on the next words; "your new queen." Placing a hand on Andreas's arm I said, "My husband, your king, Andreas."

Andreas bowed with a flourish of his arm and then put his arm around me.

"Beside Pinkert is our ship's captain, Master Night. We will all be settling here. Some sooner than others. My mother and our foster will join us at a later time We look forward to meeting each of you later at Pinkert's designated time. For now though we will get to the work of making Breen for all of us. Please don't let us keep you from your work." I bowed then and the group dispersed.

"See I told you. You will make a great queen; very magnanimous," Andreas said.

"I don't even know what that means."

"You were, considerate, fair."

"Oh, magnanimous," I said trying the word.

"Yes. They are going to love us, just you wait and see."

We finished eating and Pinkert took us on a thorough tour of the fortress before taking us to into the town side of Breen. As we crossed the drawbridge my cursed chill suddenly increased. I stopped. The shock of the chill often rendered me motionless when it came on so quickly. The others stopped and I exchanged a telling gaze with Andreas.

"Why don't we show Lio the inlet?" I asked, grasping for time to pull my self together.

Andreas put his arm around me saying, "Yes, good idea," and pointed out where he thought the dock for Night's Angel should go. I leaned against him. Then he called the captain's attention down the shore toward the fishing shacks in the distance, and they talked about a possible location for a wharf there.

When I was feeling better we discussed the fishing trade as we continued into town. Lio wanted to see things up close and asked to assess the seaward side of the fortress for the possibility of a pier for his ship there. Andreas kept close, and I was glad of him. He handled the conversation while I tried to remember all that Eble, the Master of the Mystics' Academy in Mareese, had taught me about my chill and what it could mean to me. I could control the chill, but trying to see what warning it carried would have to wait until we were alone in our chambers after the day's agenda was complete.

Heads turned to us when we entered the greenway. We soon had a following as we made our way to the smithy and entered. We had insisted that Pinkert put this on our agenda before any other matter in the city. Had it not been for the smithies our assignment to take down King Harald would have been much more treacherous. There had been three smithies then. The most frightened of them had been Coop, the cooper. We lost him in his brave attack on the inner gate of the city. That attack allowed the gate to be opened so that The Five Kings Army could move in and secure the city. We owed them our respects.

Simo and Vance dropped their work and greeted us heartily.

"Well about time, you two," Vance shouted and came to shake our hands. Simo said nothing at first but hugged us both greatly. For most of my previous time in Breen I had posed as a boy and worked for the smithies. Simo had taken us under his wing and acted like a father to us both, so it did not surprise me when Simo said, "My boys, my boys." We laughed and Simo wiped a tear.

We made introductions and shared the events of our separate roles in the coup before announcing our marriage. Pinkert moved us along shortly after. We were tardy for a meeting with the men of the guard.

We were stopped along the way by a citizen who had been in our squad during the coup. He was proud of his involvement and wanted us to meet his family; his wife and child. We spoke briefly, but Pinkert was impatient. We asked where he lived and promised a visit as soon as Pinkert's agenda gave us the time.

The rest of the day was spent greeting our soldiers, both in the city and back at the fortress. The men looked to Pinkert for approval and it was obvious that he had worked to establish his command in our absence.

He spoke to the men, "I know that you have all been anxious to meet your new king and now a queen. They are kind and noble of heart. I expect you will give them the same respect and courtesies that you have offered to me. Gentlemen, give your allegiance to King Andreas and his Queen, Saeede."

"Hail!" they yelled, and to a man they placed their hands over their hearts.

I wished they hadn't done that. It meant I would have to live up to expectations. I had never aspired to being a queen.

Andreas though, was puffed up with pride. Appropriate reactions I supposed, a proud king and his humble wife. I wondered how long we would be able to fill those roles for them.

We knew that true allegiance had to be earned. We would strive to do that everyday.

We remembered some of them from their roles in the coup. We acknowledged them, but not their involvement. Others were known to us from our time at the pub during the planning time of the coup. I got some sideways glances as they tried to settle in their minds my likeness to that of the boy recently in the employ of the smithies. Of course I was that boy, but they could arrive at their own conclusions. It did not matter to me what those conclusions were. If I was ever asked I would answer. I was not asked on that day.

We stayed a long time at the barracks in conversation about what could bring the city a more stable existence. Pinkert wrote it all down on loose sheets of vellum stacked within a leather sleeve.

When we weren't meeting soldiers we were meeting with the staff. Pinkert had them line up in the parlor of our residence. They were like soldiers at attention. Discipline was obviously important to Pinkert. If Harald had instilled it in them, then Pinkert had maintained it. I let it go, but I was not sure I would be comfortable with such strict protocol. We would have to get to know each other and see if we could relax their manner and still maintain a quality house and living.

Pinkert was there to record it all as we chatted amiably with each person, asking about relations and interests. Several entire families worked at various tasks within the house. When we had met them all Andreas asked for patience while we tried to remember all of their names. After a short speech about a better Breen and a short question and answer period we returned to our rooms. Pinkert relayed the agenda for the afternoon. We would meet with the captains of the guard and the staff managers individually. After, we would have dinner together.

"Is that how life is going to be here in Breen?" Andreas asked.

"Not if I can help it. We needed to find the right people to be in charge after Pinkert returns home to Nagrom. Someone we can trust, someone like Pinkert to oversee it all. I hope that person emerges soon. I'd like to have them under Pinkert's wing until we return."

"Yes. Now, on a topic near and dear to me; how do you feel? Is the chill still upon you?"

"Yes, sadly it is. I have it well in hand for now. I'd like to see if I can tell what it forebodes, as Eble tried to teach me back in Mareese."

"I will see that we are not disturbed," Andreas offered.

"Good. I will begin when that is done."

I sat in the center of the parlor floor with my legs crossed and my arms resting on my thighs. Andreas went to the guards at each of two doors and gave his order. I emptied my thoughts of all but myself and the chill. I had to brace myself against it. I forced my mind to look beyond it, to find a conduit of energy that was leveled at me.

I succeeded, but so briefly that it was of little help. I felt a despair so great that I instinctively reeled away from it. I immediately regretted that and endeavored to reconnect, but I was feeling overwhelmed and it was difficult to concentrate. I struggled to stay at it and finally I touched that feeling of despair again. These words came to my mind: "He waits for you again." I struggled to maintain the feeling, but no thread of it remained with me. It was gone but for the memory of it, like a dream. I turned my mind back to controlling the chill.

I gathered myself up and locked the chill back as best I could. Then I told Andreas of the experience.

"What do you think it means?"

"I have no idea. I guess part of this cursed chill will be to antagonize me with unknowable babble. Eble seemed convinced that I could foresee things through it. I was never successful under his tutelage. He said that was because we had called the chill and it had not been sent upon me as it was today. I will try again later. For now that has left me feeling drained. I think I will rest until we are called upon again."

"Good idea. While you rest I am going to go about and see what more there is of this place that Pinkert didn't show us. I wonder, for instance, if there are other secret ways within these walls."

"Will you be okay without me?"

"I will do my best. Rest now. There is not much more time before Pinkert will return with our leaders."

***

The meal with the household leaders went well. We became comfortable with each other and they came to know what we expected. When the meal was through and thay had all gone, Pinkert asked to speak with us alone.

He had a leather folder full of papers with him as he almost always did. We soon found out this one was not his. He discovered it during an audit of the depository that was secure within the fortress walls. Most of the citizens kept their valuables there in locked and guarded boxes within a guarded room inside the fortress. He could not account for the owner of one box and ordered it to be opened. There was only one thing inside—the folder that Pinkert presented to us now.

The leather dossier was stuffed with notes. Andreas and I paged through them as Pinkert spoke.

Pinkert explained, "There was no real order to the contents when I found it, but I was able to find order as I sorted through it. From what I have gathered I have no doubts this belonged to the assassin, Lily.

"She has a brillant mind, but she seems intent on doing evil with it. There are notes on the purpose of Hell and all kinds of fanatical ramblings about that. She has a particular interest in necromancy, not as a practitioner, but more as a study. I can't determine why she is so interested. Perhaps something to do with torture or assassination.

"The bulk of it is a study; that when put together reads like a diary."

It was soon obvious that this was Lily's journal. Her notes filled in things that eluded us even though we had successfully saved The Seven Kingdoms of Ahnges. After her escape and knowing her expertise at disguise we wondered if she was really the niece of King Harald of

Breen. Andreas and I never trusted our findings even after an investigation at the time confirmed that she was. We often wondered what she could have falsified. We even thought it was possible she had killed the real Lily and taken her place, She was that talented at her craft. When she referred to Harald as uncle in the notes we finally accepted that she was his niece. Lily found King Harald to be simple and only tolerated him as a convenience to her way of life.

She was approached by someone she simply called Devil. Devil wanted her to take on a task as a favor to someone called Tempter. Only a few years ago we thought my father was the king of Hell—the Dark One. We knew devil as a word like human; a race of evil beings. Now there comes this one called Devil by name. So who was the king then; what was my father's place in the hierarchy of Hell?

Tempter had the plan to undermine the kings of Ahnges and take it for himself. Without Breen Lily would have to make a place for herself somewhere. She liked the idea of being the high king's assassin, even if that king was a devil She agreed to do Tempter's dirty work. Her want to be in Hell's inner circle was becoming a reality.

Lily acted under orders from Devil but she is told that Tempter accepts her gladly. ... "as if he expected me," Lily notes. Her orders within the larger plot brought her to Mareese to assassinate Esporanza, the visiting ambassador sent by King Frahn of Nagrom.

Esporanza was the target she sought for Tempter's plan to bring down The Seven Kings but I was also a target. Not to be assassinated, but captured and turned over to Tempter. Who was Tempter and what did he want with me?

The plan to have my mother arrested was a plan to draw me away from the main course of justice and get me to work an investigation of my own. The plan nearly worked, but it was ill conceived and she never found the right time to take me. I was never really alone. Andreas was always near or just moments away.

Her plan to kill Esporanza worked but we chased her to Breen and captured her there.

"Any ideas who Tempter might be," Andreas asked of both of us.

Pinkert simply shrugged. I replied, "Another of my father's minions, out for revenge?"

"Likely," Andreas said.

"Likely that he had influence over Narhan as well."

Her uncle was no concern to her, so when the plot to over throw the kings ultimately failed she killed him and escaped our custody. Then she and Narhan, left the continent leaving the Kingdoms of Yer and Breen without a king.

"Well looks like we had it wrong after all." Andreas said.

"Yes, the plot was to take all the kings. If Tempter wanted me so badly why didn't they take me when we were in Yer."

"We didn't stay long." Andreas said.

"Yes but we would have if he had been sociable."

"Perhaps you are right that he was being controlled by this Tempter." Pinkert said. "Later in the notes; when Tempter arrives in Yer he is angry at her failure. She describes him as a creature of shadow and he freightened her very much. Narhan is already half mad, but after Tempter arrives he becomes more lucid. She calls his actions calculated.

Pinkert's words struck me with an idea. Could my father who was called The Dark One be so named for his ability to be as a shadow? Was it possible he wasn't dead? If the devil has her working in this Tempter's behalf could it be that he is not a minion to my father, but is, actually my father; himself a minion of the devil? If that was true than my father was a favorite of the High Devil, King of Hell. It explained why there was interest in me. There was no consistent thread to confirm this but the chill ran up my spine and stayed there.

"So where is Narhan? What would Tempter want with him after his plan failed?" I asked.

"He likely killed him," Andreas said.

Pinkert advised us; "There are notes in there about your quest for the Gate Scrolls. It seems she has had her eyes on the two of you for quite sometime. Did you really exterminate wild magic in a mage academy?" he asked.

"We did." Andreas boasted.

The implications that Lily had known about us long before we knew of her weighed heavily on us. Had she been conspiring with Devil all that time or with my father, a devil's minion called The Dark One? If so, why? She never made that clear. Perhaps there were more notes some where.

"I thought we were done with her!" Andreas cried.

"I need to get a message to Diony. She needs to know. She needs to keep Mam and Mya even closer. And, the kings need to know there was more to the plot to take them down. They need to know it may not have been Narhan at all!" I said.

"Right, Pinkert can you see to that?" Andreas asked. "I don't want to send Nights back yet. We will need him here to see to the business of the wharfs."

"Of course. I will do it now. Send for me if you have need of anything else."

"We will," I said, "and thank you Pinkert for finding this and bringing it to our attention. I wish we didn't have to send you back to King Frahn."

"I appreciate the sentiment, but my life is in Nagrom."

"Yes, and though we have need of you here awhile longer we will do all that we can to see you home again soon."

"Thank you, M'lord, M'lady." With that he bowed and left us alone to examine and consider the rest of Lily's report.

The contents covered many different topics. We found recipes for metallurgy, but we didn't have the experience to know what the alloy was. One recipe called for spirit blood another for blood of the insane. There had to be some magic involved—some very dark magic to bind blood with metal, but there was no instruction about that. We would have a visit with Vance, the blacksmith and see what he had to say about it.

Several sheets were written in a foreign language. It was not the ancient Arcane. Neither of us could decipher it. We called Pinkert back but he was also at a loss.

There were several detailed maps: Mareese, my Mam's shop, the Mage Academy, Breen, and Nagrom. These all seemed related to the assassination of Esporanza and her plan to kidnap me.

Our speculation of who Lily was reached into our current dilemma. If we imagined that she was working for my father, then why go after Esporanza? We needed to know about Tempter. Was that just a name she gave to King Narhan so as not to implicate him in the plot if her notes were ever discovered? Was Esporanza just a fortunate circumstance in the plan to control Ahnges, or was Esporanza just a fortunate circumstance of the plan to capture me?

Lily was still out there somewhere. Was she in Breen, or Mareese? Perhaps she felt bested and had really just gone away. Maybe she was licking her wounds in Hell. We had so much to consider and so much to accomplish. My chill grew as we looked over everything. I sat back and tried to discern what it meant, but I was tired and my head was spinning from all the new information. I could tell nothing from it.

We went to bed, but neither of us slept well. Our sleep was full of nightmares of something dark trailing us. Andreas was haunted by a fear that he could not protect me. I fought the fear of death and it came in many forms in those dark dreams.

The next day we went about the business of rebuilding Breen. We took some time out to see Vance and ask him about the metallurgical recipes. He had never seen or heard about anything like them.

That night we pulled out Lily's notes and tried to learn more about her and her plans. If she knew about the quest for the scrolls did she also know about the orb? We found no exact mention of it, but she was interested in relics of a holy and unholy nature. We cross referenced with Andreas's transcription of Eindal's ledger. There were some similarities, but where Eindal had theories and details she just had a simple list. She would have had time to make that list just after the murder, but she would have had little time for much else. We noted that the scrolls were mentioned but the orb was not. That made us feel a little safer. There was little reason to believe that she sought the orb Still, Lily was becoming a nemesis. We had to assume that she knew everything about us and everything we did.

We packed the notes away with the other gear we expected to take with us. The notes were safe in the false leather bottom of the carpetbag.

We turned our focus solely on Breen after that, so we could get on to the business of retrieving the orb.

***

We spent three weeks locked into our duties as the rightful leaders of Breen. I began calling Andreas, Potentate. A title he found rather annoying, but I found quite fun.

Potentate and I rode the borders, met with the household, balanced the books, and saw to the purchase of supplies for Captain Nights pier and the fishermen's wharf.

Nights found a suitable spot for his ship's pier. It was well situated on the seaward side of the fortress just as he had hoped. A stairway and board walk would be built from the pier to the main gate until a rear gate could be built for direct access.

Nights designed the wharf to be expandable as commerce increased. The first pilings were being driven into the sand before we left.

Construction of pier and wharf would continue while we were away. The captain chose several local tradesmen to work on them. Much of the supplies would be harvested or manufactured by our own people and they were glad of the work and the money we would pay them for it.

We visited often with the proud coup member and hired him to be our head of house when Pinkert went home to Nagrom. Enot, his pregnant wife, Otta, and their boy child, Enta moved into quarters at the fortress and were soon beloved members of the staff. That was a good thing, because they were expected to keep our staff happy and healthy in our absence. They would answer only to us, or to Pinkert while we were away.

We often went about town to ask the shop owners and families what we could do to make Breen flourish. At the end of three weeks we had some good ideas and began to implement what we could afford. When we had time to rest we spent it at the pub and got to know our soldiers.

Things were looking good for Breen and the citizen's were happy and anxious to participate in the changes. With the business of Breen well in hand we advised Pinkert that we had been called upon to squelch a situation in Koman.

"Does it have anything to do with those notes of Lily's?" he asked.

"Yes." I said impulsively. It wasn't exactly true but at that time I wasn't ready to exclude Lily either.

We assured him that it might affect us all later if it wasn't seen to. He did not question us on the matter and agreed to stay on to oversee the whole of our interests until our return.

We wanted to let the people of Breen down easily. We didn't expect our news to sit well with them. We planned a celebration. We took some of the money we had gained from Harald's coffers and ordered the staff to make a party for all of Breen's citizens. It would be held in the inner garden of the fortress.

The night of the party came and we waited in our rooms until the hum of activity in the garden was constant. We made our entrance while playing an unfinished musical piece we were calling Harald's Bane. We changed up a bit and I played Andreas's favored instrument; the mandolin, while Andreas played mine; the flute. If they weren't already, the crowd was fond of us then. The people cheered and laughed with glee. We walked amongst them and played several light tunes that caused them to dance and sing.

Andreas was right; they loved us for all we had done and who we were. We had won them over and so that night, as was our plan, we announced our departure.

They were dismayed. There was the expected grumbling, but we assured them of our return. We told them that we were called away on a matter of grave importance to the known world. If they knew how grave they would have run away to hide. We emphasized that if it was not dealt with the consequences could be dire for all of us later on.

Fortunately our reputation as wardens for the common good served to keep them on our side. Their displeasure at having us leave so soon turned to pride for a king and queen who were so able to keep them safe. I hoped that we could live up to their expectations.

We left the next morning and rode to Nagrom. Lio Nihoc had gone ahead of us to return the wagon and gather his crew. When we arrived we went straight to the Night's Angel. We did not wait for the tides to turn, but slipped neatly away from the docks under Captain's orders and sailed west along the southern coast of Dinar and then turned north to Koman.

·~·Chapter Four·~·

I spent most of the trip in our accommodation below deck. It was not seasickness that was upon me this time. The chill had taken a greater hold on the day that we pulled away from the harbor of Nagrom. I expended great energy to keep it at bay and to determine what warning it had for me. I was not as sure as Eble the mystic, that I could foretell future events through some power of the chill. I tried none-the-less.

Several times I felt the touch of despair again. In that touch, a thought; *'He waits for you.'* Sometimes the words brought a horrible fear and the chill felt as if it would stop my heart. Whoever delivered the words upon my mind was gentle though, like a fond memory. I never got a sense for what it meant So many conflicting emotions barraged me. I could not be sure that what Eble thought was glimmers of prescience were really just the ravings of my rattled frozen mind.

Weeks passed on that ship and I was wholly frustrated by the time we reached the island country of Koman.

Koman was a grey span of ice covered granite. The mountains piled up from the steep shore and rose higher and higher toward the center of the large island. Rich minerals lay deep in those mountains. The city of Koman was situated on a small bay on the east side of the island. There was no harbor large enough for Night's Angel to maneuver in rough seas so two men rowed us ashore. The waves tossed us so we joined our efforts with theirs to get to shore. They dropped us off and returned immediately to the ship. I did not envy them the trip. Nights would sail east and anchor a few miles out in the strait between Ahnges and Koman. He supplied us with a lantern and some oil so that we could signal him. When we were ready to return he would send the dinghy to pick us up.

The city smelled; a great stinking conglomerate smell of waste, fish, sea, and garbage. The citizens crept about as if Death haunted them. Perhaps he did. We had no desire to stay among such people. We spoke to the first person we found, a young woman, to get directions to the asylum. She backed away from us and pointed toward a mountain peak that loomed over the forsaken city. We looked back to thank her, but she was gone; slipped away without a sound.

We left town immediately, but a dirty little, pointy nosed man with grey skin slipped out of a shadow and blocked our way at the edge of town. "You seek the mountain, and the asylum there. Do you have someone there? I can take you. The way is twisty and you will get lost without a guide."

"You seem awfully sure of that," Andreas said. "How can you be?"

"Many have gone, but never return. Evil lives there. Everyone knows it. Some say the gate to Hell is through the asylum. I don't know about that, but I have no desire to enter in where those wickedly insane reside. People here wrestle with insanity. There are all sorts of stories, things steal people away at all times of day and night. The spirits of demons drive them out of their minds and into the dark. They all end up in the asylum. Evil begins there—evil lives there."

"What sort of ghost story are you telling?" Andreas demanded.

"No story, but I will tell you one. After, you must decide if you will hire me as your guide. If you do I will tell you all the stories you can stand to hear."

"Tell me first what you want for wages should we decide to take you along."

"Four pieces of gold. One for each day of travel. Two in and two back; I will not charge you for the time I will wait for you to return."

"Tell us your story."

"Not here."

"Where then?"

The man turned without a word and pointed down a thin alley between two decrepit homes.

"We aren't falling for that," Andreas said. We moved aside of him to continue on our way.

The man moved to blocked our way again. This time our hands drew weapons.

"No, no," the man said. "No need for such harsh actions. I should have seen you were no fools and would not follow me along that route. It is the way to my house, that's all. But I will walk with you and tell my story as promised in hopes that you will give me gainful employment.

We had no intention of hiring him, but remembered Eindal's mention of a man he had contact with on Koman. Perhaps they had met that very same way. Perhaps this was that man. I listened intently. Local stories often carry more information than even the teller knows.

As he began to tell his tale my chill increased. I could not be certain what warning it gave, or if it was linked to that smarmy man. I pushed the chill back and focused on the man.

He was saying; "It all started when some fool messed with the Hell Gates. Many devils and demons came up then. All things that comes from the asylum that ain't human is black; or so dark green, or blue, or purple, as to seem black. Some has wings, they are the leaders. All manner of wings, but mostly they is dark too.

There was a battle here then. Great bright soldiers fought against the dark devils. One dark winged devil commander paced the lands 'tween the asylum and the dark army. The bright army tried to drive them back, but there was too many of the dark army and the bright army fled.

"The dark army collected the spoils strewn across the battlefield. When the leader found something there was a commotion. The dark army swarmed around him. When he emerged he had with him a soldier

39

of the bright army. It was so absolutely beatific and full of light; like an angel. It didn't have wings, but it was tall, very tall like the winged demon.

When the man described the captured creature I could think only of the word that Andreas had used on our voyage from Mareese-- synchronous. More angels; I was dumbfounded. Why here and not in heaven where they belonged?

I realized that I was staring at the man when he said, "They bound it all up in the blackest chains; what could only be argentinus.

Andreas spoke through his own bewilderment. "Argentinus?" Andreas asked, and we shared a knowing look. It was one of the metallurgic recipes found in Lily's notes. The one that used the blood of the insane as an ingredient.

"A rare metal forged by the devil's smith and imbued with evil. We know of it here, 'cause they uses it on the sane. Even the best of folks is rendered helpless when touched by it. We calls it Bane Metal." The man said.

"Did you see this yourself, or are you telling me some horror story told around the nighttime fires?"

"I saw it myself. The devils have no fear of us. They make their homes somewhere beneath the asylum. They find no reason to hide from us. We are prey to them."

"Your story asks more questions than it answers. We are in need of answers. I am afraid we cannot use your services."

"You will be lost in a day," he said.

"We will take our chances," Andreas replied.

"I will only charge you half, and still I will see you safely there."

"Why are you so anxious to lead us?"

The man answered quickly, "Money is hard to come by here. I see an opportunity and I need to take it, to buy passage off this forsaken place. Not many ships dock here. When they do their price to take on a

Komanian is high. I need the money to get out of here before I am next for the asylum."

I took Andreas's arm and moved him out of earshot of the man. "His request seems reasonable," I said, but Andreas shot me a wary look. I continued, "Don't you think this could be the contact that Eindal had here? Perhaps Eindal was approached in the same way."

"I assumed the same. If that is so, why is he still here? Eindal was known to be a charitable man. If this guy used that story on him surely Eindal would have taken care of it.

"Most likely, let's see."

We turned and walked back to the man who watched us warily.

Andreas took up the conversation where it had left off. "You might say anything to get us out of town and kill us for what we carry in this carpetbag, since you are so desperate for coin."

"No Master, Sir, no. It is only as I say."

"You expect us to trust you to take us into unknown territory? Territory brimming with evil creatures if I am to believe your story. We don't even know you."

"Apologies; I am called Jest. I assure you, I am harmless. I make my way with odd jobs. One of those is offering guide services to strangers. The last two years has seen a decline in visitors and so too my savings."

Andreas and I shared a suspicious look. Neither of us was sure what to do with this man. "You mean since the horde wars down south?" I asked.

"Especially since then, though Koman has never been a great vacation spot way up here in the cold sea."

"Have you ever heard the name Eindal?" I ventured, I was anxious to be done with the man and be on our way.

He turned to look at me with something akin to hatred. I took it as fear and suspicion. Then he looked at Andreas with renewed interest as well. "I don't know you either, why should I tell you who I know." he said.

"And yet you were so eager to talk only moments ago. I will put that in the yes column. You knew Eindal" Andreas said.

"Nor should you know us," I said. "Eindal sent us." I lied, but the words rang true to my reasoning. Had it not been for the ledger we would not have been there.

"Why has he not come himself?" Again, that look came over his face.

"It was Eindal's dying wish that we come and procure an item for the sake of humanity."

A look of doubt flashed in his eyes, but was gone as quickly. His voice shook nervously when he asked; "When, how? I warned him he was in too deep when he came up here asking about Hell Gates and such." Then a dawn of realization came across his face. "You are going into Hell to retrieve an item for a dead man?"

"In a manner of speaking, yes.

"Now that we know who you are, we know you were Eindal's contact here. Did he ever mention an orb?" I asked.

"You are fools. You will not survive the Hells. One of those demons alone can look you dead if they wants it."

"Let us worry about that." Andreas said. "The lady asked you about an orb."

"Azure orb, yeah I heard, but I knows nothin' 'bout sech a thing."

"Who said it was azure?" I asked. I watched the man's reactions. He was nervous, since the mention of Eindal's name and more so since we mentioned the orb. I imagined I would be nervous too if Hell was in my back yard and strangers came along to stir it up, but he knew more than he was telling, and had just tripped over it.

I knew Andreas felt the same way when he took up again, "You fear the asylum yet you offer to take us to it, and then wait, alone. Aren't you afraid you might be caught by one of the black creatures that roam about? They might eat you."

That thought caused the man some fear, but he said, "I has found me a good hidey hole."

"Couldn't they smell you? You would be trapped there in your hole. They would only have to reach in and grab you." At that Andreas reached out and grabbed the man by the collar.

The man did not move and looked dismayed. "Eindal was a good man. He was benevolent towards me and the people here."

"He has that reputation. I wonder why he didn't book safe passage off of this island for you. Maybe he didn't trust you."

"Tell us what you know about the orb," I said.

"He is sending you on a suicide mission. You shouldn't go."

"The orb. Tell us."

"Eindal asked about it. That is how I know. That is all I know."

Andreas held the man for a long moment trying to assess the danger he might bring on us. He thought little of it and released him. "Go away little man. I do not trust you. We will find the way. If you leave us alone, then on our return I will give you five gold for your savings. In memory of Eindal. Go now," Andreas said.

Jest did not move, so Andreas lunged at him. He moved then, turning as quick as could be to run down the alley that led to his home.

We moved then too and made our way toward the mountains with weapons drawn from then on.

"Do you think we should have scared him away?" I asked.

"Did you have use of him?"

"No. I just wonder what more he has to tell."

"If we need him we know where to find him."

***

43

We could see the tallest mountain at the center of the island. The asylum would be there. Each time we found a path that seemed to lead to it we were blocked by stone or precipice and we were forced to turn back and find another way.

We crawled over the mountains for a week narrowly escaping several encounters. We were not so lucky with several more. Each beast we faced was different. Some walked upright like Men, but had characteristics of animals; one had fur, another scales. One beast had a head like that of a horse, but with teeth like a lion, and the bite was severe. There were those beasts that snarled and growled like cats or dogs. We knew of their coming, but they attacked in packs and they were clever. We never learned their strategy. One or two would mark us and howl to their pack. The pack never came from the same direction as the howlers. We could not turn our attention from any direction during those encounters because the attacks never followed a pattern.

There were beasts that crawled upon their bellies like reptiles. They liked to hide in the cracks of stones or along ledges, or in the trees. Often they had small wings or great hind legs so they could leap to their attack. I think I feared these the most. They were difficult to battle as they leaped about and surprised us often.

It seemed that the more we battled the more we were attacked. Those beasts in mountains knew we were there. We were lucky to be alive at all and our supply of healing unguent was low.

It was an odd relief when we stumbled into a path leading directly to the front gate of the asylum. We scrambled back into the cover of rocks and shadows as quickly as we could and peered cautiously over the rocks that hid us.

The place was so ordinary in appearance and construction that it seemed out of place in those oily, grey stone mountains. The path curved pleasantly up to a wrought iron gate with a wrought iron arch above. A fence; also of wrought iron enclosed a courtyard that was pleasant enough. Stone benches were arranged under a few tangled trees that grew there. A stout two story manse constructed of local stone was situated in the center of the yard. Efflorescence covered wide swathes of the stone with white powder. Thin arched windows looked out at precise spacing all around on both floors. Every window was covered with grids of latticed iron, bolted firmly through the stone walls The entrance was set back between two flanking wings of the building and another wrought iron fence and gate spanned that space. Beyond that gate, stone steps led up to a single door of weathered wood.

There was no one in the courtyard and no sentries at the gates. We stayed a long time watching and the yard remained empty. From time to time a resident would come to peer out a window. They seemed docile for the most part, but one screeched at the window as he scratched at the iron lattice. He went on until his fingers bled and then retreated, sobbing, to the interior of the building.

We had no chance of entering without being seen during the grey daylight hours, so we moved into better cover and waited for the dark of night. We did not sleep and watched the asylum for activity and our surroundings for attack. We spoke not at all, not even a whisper from fear that we would be discovered. My chill was well under control and oddly; it diminished the longer we stayed outside the asylum. I could not seem to come to grips with what the chill was supposed to be telling me. Perhaps it was telling me I was on the right trail. I dared not try to divine again to know better what the chill foretold so close to an entrance to Hell. I feared that I might trigger its evil and that would be like a beacon. I could rely only on my own wits and skills—mine and Andreas's.

When last we entered Hell we had the support of a church and the church's paladins, an army of contracted mercenaries, and a network of spies, theologians, and politicians. This time it was just we two; alone. Alone.

Night came too quickly, when it did we moved reluctantly to the gate, and peered through the bars. In the shadows of the mountains not even the light of the moon reached us. The house though, seemed to glow. The salts brought to the surface of the masonry, had fluorescent qualities. The courtyard was cast in a low eerie light. We would be able to navigate without aid of torchlight.

Andreas reached to test the gate and reeled from an unnatural shock that it sent through him. It left no mark, but his arm was numb for a long time and he reported that his ears rang with a shrill sound and his head hurt behind his eyes. We waited for his pains to subside and then I tested the gate. I reasoned that in a place of devils and demons the blood of my father might protect me. I was right.

I worked my talent for picking locks and tested the action of the hinges. They were tight and would creak if opened too far. We used a few drops of Captain Night's oil on the hinges and worked it in slowly until we were able to open the gate enough to slip through without a sound. We were through the first gate unaccosted.

I pushed the gate closed and saw no choice but to relock it. We did not want an unlocked gate to call attention to our arrival.

Andreas returned his staff-sword to its harness at his left shoulder. He picked up the carpetbag to cradle it in his arms and keep it from jangling as we ran across the yard to the wide building entrance.

There were no traps, the qualities of the metal were deterrent enough for normal people. We oiled the hinges as a precautionary measure and I went to work to unlock it.

What did someone do who had a loved one housed inside? They could not enter in without great pain and risk to their own sanity. Those poor souls inside would be left alone to fend off the sins evil played out against them. Both the incarcerated and the free were held captive by the same evil. I was beginning to form a theory about the workings of that place. If Bane Metal was enough to render good people insane;

perhaps the asylum was more like a depository. I wondered, could someone be rendered so insane that they could be turned to evil? If unleashed and allowed to roam the island what would they inflict upon their own people? My thoughts raced; one phasing into another. How many demons had gone off the island? Had that become easier with aid of God's Iris?

I refocused my attention on the business at hand. The oil did its work. The cams of the lock turned and the latch transit pulled the latch in smoothly. The gate popped open and we slipped in. I pushed the gate closed and relocked it.

The enclosure between the wings of the mansion was a series of short stairs and landings that filled the space. Andreas carried the carpet bag in his left hand and took the staff-sword back into his right. The bag could be easily dropped if we needed to defend ourselves.

Up the stairs we went. We did not check for wards or traps. Who but us would be crazy enough to pass willingly into so menacing a place? The Bane Metal alloy in the fences would be enough to deter ordinary folks.

At the door I listened. I could hear the distant sounds of moaning, sobbing, insane laughter, and something else I could not discern.

I looked at Andreas. He was tense. I was tense. I grabbed him and kissed him, a passionate kiss that he returned. It might be the last time I would ever be able to do that. I did not allow my fear to steal that from me.

"I love you too," he whispered. "Let's get this over with so we can go home."

The door was locked, but easily undone, it opened to an opulent vestibule. A fireplace spanned the right-hand wall and a gathering of settee and chairs were set before it. Thick red velvet curtains with gold tassels were closed across the windows and clashed with the garish green and yellow material of the furniture. Paintings of bizarre and obscene subject matter hung crooked on the wall. That room which was meant to welcome visitors as they awaited attendance by an official was appalling and not welcoming at all.

To our left an opening gave access to an equally garish arrangement of furniture in a dusty library. The curtains matched those of the vestibule, except that they were open. Another opening in the vestibule allowed us into a foyer with a sweeping stairway to the upper floor. The sounds of moaning, sobbing, and insane laughter, came from upstairs. The something else thrummed all around us. We were uninterested in going up. As we all know Hell is down.

From the foyer we could see into the library, a dining room, and a hall that led to a busy kitchen and a small closet.

The closet had no door or contents. What it did have was a small square door halfway up the wall. I examined it and had it opened quickly. Inside was a small elevator. I had seen one used during our stay in Kapit's holding's in Behlanna; it was used to transport meals and linens between floors. The platform moved easily and down was an option. If we sat on the platform we could run the ropes and move up or down between the floors of the asylum.

We climbed in before anyone could come from the kitchen and discover us. I wondered if they worked in such a place willingly or if they were pathetic drones who had lost all their senses. I did not want to have to harm someone like that if they cried out. I was certain their silence could not be purchased, and any skirmish at all was unacceptable at this early time in our entrance.

Andreas lowered us slowly and quietly. The platform went down one floor to the basement and stopped just short of the floor. There was no surrounding shaft on this floor and we could see that the basement was a wide open space beneath the asylum.

We climbed off of the platform and after returning the elevator to its start position we began our search for a way deeper into the mountain.

·~·Chapter Five·~·

With the elevator platform back in the closet above us the space was broken only by the thick stone columns placed equally to support the mansion above us.

No gates to Hell that we could see.

That was the problem it couldn't be seen. As I stepped about the space I walked under the elevator and into an invisible portal. I heard Andreas gasp as I fell through, then a second later he jumped through behind me.

We landed on a stone dais in the middle of a desolate landscape. The stone below us vibrated and the thrumming that it made was that which we had heard all around us in the asylum.

Above us was a red sky. Below us was red sand. The black stone of the dais stood out in stark contrast to all that we could see. We were two vulnerable mortals suddenly appearing on Hell's threshold. We jumped down a short distance and crouched against the dais.

A survey of all directions showed that in all directions but one, there was nothing but hot red sand and red sky. Only one direction showed a change in elevation and color. The red sky faded to a more familiar blue. The elevated land showed a faint blue, much like the hills on our homeland of Crystalier showed from a distance. Our choice was obvious. We moved out quickly in the direction of the hills.

It was not long before the sand rose up and fell away to reveal two shadowy resemblances of ourselves. They leaped upon us before we could check our amazement. We took them quickly, but two more rose up just as quickly. Those two were harder to vanquish, but we did. As they fell two more rose up. These fought quite well and they gave us several wounds before they fell to us. Again two more, and this time we were equally matched. They had learned our moves from each previous battle and they seemed to anticipate our actions. They were fresh and we were beginning to fade. Desperate that we could not win; we ran.

A quick fake and lunge and we were passed them, sprinting toward the rising land. They gave chase and were gaining on us when Andreas stopped and blew out his breath. The sand all around us rose up and swirled before him. The doppelgängers slowed, wondering at this phenomenon. One called out in a discomfiting voice, "You cannot defeat us."

"We'll see about that," Andreas said, and sent the whirl of sand forward like a great spear of sand. With another breath he increased the speed and force behind it.

It was their turn to run, but they could not move quick enough. The force hit them and broke their backs. Their effort to mimic our forms faded with the onslaught of their pain. They changed to their true forms; black faceless things with webbed hands and feet sprawled upon the ground. They cried out in agony. We went to them and ran them through with our blades. The act may have given mercy but there was no meditation of it. We did what we did to silence them. Their blood turned the sand around us black. I muttered a prayer, but my heart was not in it.

Andreas swirled the sand beneath them until they sank down to the clay below. The sand settled over them until we could see no difference from that spot and the sands around us. We ran back to the site of the other encounters, and gave the same treatment to those who had fallen there.

Our wounds needed tending. We saved the unguent for critical or festering wounds. For now we just needed to stop the bleeding. We had to take the time but we watched constantly for movement in the sand. It disturbed us to think that we could be walking or standing over dark creatures at anytime.

After our wounds were bound we ran; a desperate pace that was difficult to maintain, but gave us an advantage over anything that could rise up from nothing to fight against us. Fear of what might lie beneath us at every step urged us forward.

We were closing in on the welcoming hills. As we approached them I surged ahead, anxious to reach them. Andreas pushed too and the race was on. The edge of the sand was just ahead.

Without warning, a great maw opened before us. A sand serpent; perfectly blended with the sand, sensed the pounding of our feet to open at just the right moment. We could not stop. We were in it and swallowed.

Strong throat muscles closed in around us. Thick ribs pushed against us and we were helpless to swing weapons. We choked on the bile of the beast as he swallowed and we moved closer to the stomach. I managed to get my blade up in front of me in a moment when the muscles relaxed between swallows. I pushed up into the space and pierced the throat and the meat of the thing. The beast jerked and we were thrown against the wall and the ribs of the throat. I managed an awkward stab at the thing from under my arm and pierced the throat again. The snake convulsed. I fell, dragging the blade down through the flesh. The serpent gasped and opened its mouth. We pushed our way through convulsing muscle and stumbled out of the huge mouth.

The serpent laid still and gasping. Andreas dropped the carpetbag and opened the side of the beast with his staff-sword in two hands. We left it to die.

I bent to examine the red sand. It seemed as if the sand itself could conjure these monsters. I took some sand in one hand and let it sift through my fingers as I wondered over that. A soft wind lifted it and it swirled away.

"I dub thee The Desert of Desperation," I whispered.

"Funny, I was thinking the same." Andreas said. "Lets get out of here." We took up our run again, until we stood on top of the nearest hill. Once there we flopped down to rest and drink.

·~·Chapter Six·~·

Up until then my experiences with Hell had been filled with eerie landscapes. The view at the top of the hills was nothing like that. The hills rolled and were covered with thick velvety moss. From where we stood we could see beyond the next hill to a kettle valley. A lake twinkled at the bottom of the valley. Across the valley the hills rolled as far as our eyes could see. At the horizon a blue sky touched the lush green hills.

The sight confused us. It was as if we had crossed out of Hell and back onto Earth, but Koman had no landscape like that. The beauty made us more afraid of the place than we already were. We did not know if what we saw was real. We checked our weapons, took another mouthful of water and went to look over the rim into the valley.

A village was built on boardwalks along the nearest walls of the valley and wooden causeways crossed the water to an elliptical pier in the center of the lake. The buildings were like those in any cozy fishing village, but there was no life. We saw no creatures milling about on the causeways or near the buildings. Perhaps they slept. On the central pier was a wooden temple. To what devil-god we did not know and it would not matter. We would face whatever evils were in store no matter where they came to face us.

On the side of the pier furthest from us a bridge branched across the water and led to an opening at the root of the hills on the other side of the lake. We hoped that opening ran deeper into the depths of Hell. Such a dark hope—to be glad of a way into the deeps of Hell. We were being beckoned to it, like in a nightmare, when you are compelled to follow that which has you terrified. From our vantage point we could see no way down to that opening if we approached from the other side.

Near by to us a stairway cut out of the hill led down to the village edge. Andreas walked to them and took a few steps down. The hump of the hill into which the stairs were cut would keep us hidden until we reached the boardwalk. We went down together. The fear of ambush kept us both taut and ready to defend, but no ambush came. We moved through the village sideways, back to back. We came to the central pier and no attack had come.

We could hear a low hum coming from inside the temple. Abhorrent carvings covered every inch of the temple structure. I will not describe them here. The memory of them sickens and maddens me just as it did then. We had no choice but to cross and be near the temple if we were to cross the bridge.

Closer still and the hum became a chant from within the temple. The language was unknown to us, but it had an effect. The tones were so smooth and melodious that we nearly became enthralled. The chill flared up in me like a cold fire and broke the spell. Andreas was not as lucky. He shuffled helplessly toward the door. I grabbed him, but he fought me off. He reached for the door and I slapped his face as hard as I could. It worked and he came back to his senses. I grabbed him and we ran down the pier as fast as we could, before the chant could overwhelm us again.

The slap and pounding of our feet upon the piers alerted the occupants of the temple to our presence. The chanting became louder and faster. Two demons left the temple and on seeing us gave pursuit.

They stood up right like humans but their heads were like great mastiffs. When they saw us they fell to all fours and ran with the strength and speed of hounds on the hunt. If we did not turn to fight they would catch us on the bridge that crossed the lake. That did not appeal to us at all, so we turned and braced for the assault.

I had only one sword in hand. I had sheathed the other to drag Andreas from the temple. There was no time to draw the other. They leaped at us. We swung our weapons, but they brushed them aside and took us down. We hit the pier with such force that our breath was forced from us. I lost my sword on impact and could only keep the teeth of the demon off my neck with brute strength as I desperately gasped for air.

Andreas was in much the same predicament, but he had his staff-sword between him and the demon who snarled and slathered very near his neck.

After a few seconds of terror, I got my feet up under the demon-dog's belly and launched him off of me. I came to my feet and filled my lungs. My head spun, but I found my sword on the ground and went to it as I reached for the one I had sheathed.

I had made the mistake of turning my back on the creature and I was not as quick as I had thought I would be. I was wrong to think I would be able to get both weapons in hand and turn to meet another attack. The impact of his next leap hit me in the shoulders and the middle back all at once. My body arced backwards as the force of the impact took us both over the temple pier and into the dark water.

I managed to hold on to my swords, but the water prevented me from using them effectively. The beast clung to me and got his teeth into my neck. I dropped the weapons and watched them sink away as I did the only thing that I could. To keep the beast from ripping out arteries in my neck I reached around with both hands and pried open his jaw. The beast gasped for the first time and filled his lungs with water. He let go of me and swam for the surface. I followed, but I was holding my breath. I caught hold of a hind leg and yanked the beast down. He thrashed at me, but I climbed up his side and kicked off of his shoulders. I launched to the surface and he plunged away; his flailing causing him more harm than good.

I surfaced and took a ragged breath. I could not swim. I turned over and floated, kicking my way toward the pier until I could breathe normally. All the while I could hear the strains of Andreas's struggle with his assailant. When at last I was able to climb up and over the pier edge Andreas had managed to get upright. The beast fought on his hind legs and stood over Andreas by a fotmal. I drew two daggers from the crossed bandoliers at my chest and ran to his aid.

We took turns jabbing and retreating. The persistent attacks were too much and he soon fell to us. We threw him over the pier with a great splash. I replaced one dagger and snatched up the carpetbag from where it had landed precariously, one end over the edge of the pier. As I straightened up a massive form swam across my view, just below the surface. Then it dove. A black scaly tail slapped the water. Seconds later the beast rose out of the water with the demon-dog in its mouth, before submerging again. Any thoughts I had of going in after my swords were quickly amended. I opened the carpet bag and withdrew an old sword. I would be fighting with sword and dagger from then on.

"Good thing you didn't get eaten too," Andreas said as he came up beside me. "That laceration on your neck is like chum in the water. It needs tending."

"Not here. Let's get across first."

"Keep your dagger against it then. Give me the bag."

The great fish circled below the bridge. We waited a tense moment for the fish to move. When it did we ran across as fast as we could. We saw its shadowy form again, but it must have eaten its fill and it left us alone.

The pier ended just inside the dark opening. There was no gate or door to block our access. That bothered me. The only gates we had gone through were those at the asylum entrance. They had been so easy to get through. They hardly seemed like Hell gates. The portal in the basement was something altogether different, not really a gate at all. Somehow, when we returned we would have to destroy it.

The floor and ceiling of the passage sloped sharply down into the root of the hill. I got down on my knees to look under the declining ceiling, but all I saw was dark corridor. Andreas lit a torch and we stepped carefully along the smooth stone.

When we were out of site of the door and the corridor ahead was empty Andreas insisted on a rest. I held the torch as he tended to the angry rends on my neck. We took time after to rest and have a small meal of smoked meat and water before moving on.

On and on and on we went. No beast or manner of being came up or down, yet I felt as if we were swarmed by them. My chill increased and my already dim outlook on our mission grew dark and hopeless. Andreas seemed un-phased, but I felt as if tiny creatures hung on me; whispering messages of despair in my ears. It seemed as if the corridor would go on forever and I trudged on; wrestling with invisible manifestations.

Another hour passed before a pale light played upon our eyes. As we came closer we could make out a precision opening cut into the stone. No sound came from that direction and we moved to the opening.

The time it took to navigate the last length of that corridor seemed like a flash in time, though we had moved to it with the same caution we had used along its length. Dread kept us on edge. The anticipation of our next encounter left a metal taste in my mouth. Even that intensified my fear. If I could taste it I imagined the denizens of that horrific place could smell it.

Near the opening we put our backs to opposite walls and moved to peer into the room, still under cover of the dark corridor. Two more openings, like that in which we hid, stood in corners of an odd shaped ante room. Through one door a bright light fell and lit that side of the ante room. Through the other door we could make out a downward stairway into darkness.

Neither of us wanted to go any longer into the dark. Still it had to be investigated. We did not know where we were going so nothing could be ruled out. Hell is down, we reasoned. We moved out, keeping close to the near wall and followed it around to the dark stairway. Like children afraid of the dark we ran down the stairs away from the light to keep from being discovered from the room behind us. The contrariety of that action disturbed me. I felt like I had fallen into a paradox. It was not the first time that unsettling feeling came over me.

I didn't have time to dwell on it. As I moved off the stairs an unseen adversary slammed into me. The torch blew out and I was lifted into the air; not by hands but by a great force. Shadow had found me.

I was completely enveloped in darkness, but this was a warm, soothing darkness. I could feel the thing like a velvet blanket all around me. I could have slept comfortably there. If I had I surely would have died, but the chill flared again and my mind set right. From sweet oblivion to dire stress. I could not breathe. I could not move or cry out in despair; the thing had wrapped me so tight.

I could not hear Andreas and wondered if he was caught too. I could not feel his body within my wrapping. I knew that if he was safe he was doing all he could to save me. If he was caught as well, then at least we died together.

When I felt hot explosions hit and flare out along the outer surface of the shadow I was reassured. An eerie screech emitted from the thing and it let me go. I fell from the ceiling, where it had taken me. Andreas came to help me up, but never took his eyes from the ceiling.

"Let's get out of here," he said. "It's a dead-end. I can keep it away for now, but I don't know if it will get brave."

I gathered the fallen torch and returned it to the carpetbag. Then taking up the bag I touched Andreas's shoulder. We backed up the stairs. The shadow remained unseen in that dark room.

Back in the ante room Andreas kept his attention on the shadow room while I guided him toward the room of light. "Light and shadow," I whispered. "how appropriate. I'll wager what lies behind the light will be worse than that shadow."

"Keeping a positive outlook, I see," Andreas retorted.

"I am positive that what lies behind the light will be worse than that shadow."

"What do you see?"

"It's a round stairway with a central shaft. Light swirls about in the shaft. I think it comes from somewhere below. There is a landing here and stairs wrap down around either side of the light. They end at another landing. On that landing is a gate."

"At last."

"I don't understand. Where have we been all this time if not in Hell?"

"Hades? A place of tormented souls somewhere on the edge of Hell?"

"So, there *are* other ways in and out of Hell that our friends do not know. I didn't think that the invisible portal in the basement could be a gate. There was no lock."

"We will worry about that later. Let's move on now."

I stepped onto the landing and Andreas stood behind me. He still had his eyes on the shadow's lair. The air in the shaft swirled in a column of noxious mephitic vapors that filled the shaft, but did not spill onto the stairs. The gas expelled light. I had never seen anything like it, nor have I since. The swirling light made it impossible to tell if the source was above or below us. The yellow light itself was an indication of how toxic the gas that breathed through that central shaft was. If I opened that gate and we were attacked on the landing a fall into that shaft was extremely probable and absolutely deadly.

I told Andreas to wait there and went alone to the landing. This gate was different than those we had encountered so far. This was not the black Bane Metal we had encountered at the asylum. Although it had the same glassy texture; this metal was a deep blood red. I peered through the gate into utter darkness. Not even the light in the shaft penetrated beyond the gate. I saw nothing but the dark.

I remembered our first foray into Hell and the gate I had helped Andreas to open when I was out of phase. That gate had been red as well.

I touched the gate and a wave of intense agony gripped me. It was not a physical pain, but a pain of the soul. I released the bars. If I had no soul I would have suffered no ill effects. In my sardonic way I was happy to know that I had a soul. I shuddered away the darkness that had touched me.

What price had Andreas paid at that gate those years ago? I had only been able to touch it because I was out of phase—between worlds.

I looked over the lock. It was a complicated apparatus. I could avoid some contact with the gate to manipulate my tools, but the lock was deep and massive, some contact was inevitable. I did not like that idea. Instead I pulled a tune from my memory of deciphering the gate scrolls. I had serious doubts, but it was worth a try before I touched the gate again. I knelt, took my flute from the bag and began to play. The gate vibrated, but when I tested it I was shocked again by the deepest otherworldly agony. I dropped the flute and it nearly rolled into the shaft. Andreas was there to stop it.

He had come down behind me as I played and witnessed the vibration of the gate. He took his harp and checked the tuning. "You need the rest of it. We can stomp out the percussion with our feet."

I stood and we played a most eerie and wonderful composition. The gate vibrated, then hummed a crescendo that joined well with the music. Then we heard a click and the gate sprang open. We went in quickly. The gate swung back and we played until we heard the lock; even knowing the sound might attract attention. No denizens of this Hell would get by the gate while we could stand.

"Do you realize we just locked a Hell Gate with the instruments of angels?" Andreas whispered.

"The idea had not escaped me. Did you plan that? I was a little surprised when you took the harp rather than the mandolin."

"It struck me as I reached for the mandolin and there was the harp."

"Well it is a dramatic touch, I'll say that for you."

He sighed with some exasperation I had caused him, but he said nothing. He did not return the harp to the bag, but slung it by a thong over his shoulder.

It seemed wise to have our instruments near and ready if more gates blocked us. I tucked my flute into my belt.

No attack came. We took stock of our gear, making sure all was where we expected it to be. Then we looked long at each other. My heart ached when I looked at him. For years we had kept our relationship as friends, thinking loss would be easier if it came to that. It would not have been. He was my dearest and longest friend. Our marriage was but a step along the way.

He reached for me and pulled me close. We stayed that way in silence for a long time. If intelligent creatures moved about in the darkness they now knew our greatest weakness.

"Alright," Andreas whispered. "Let's go save the world one more time."

"Can you see anything?" I asked.

"Only you."

"I wish you were just being charming."

"Me too."

"I don't think we can risk a light source."

"I agree. Take my hand."

I did and he cast the staff-sword out ahead of us like a blind man. I carried the bag and one sword in the same hand, my daggers were near at hand in the bandolier across my chest. We moved forward, directly away from the gate. The surface beneath our feet crunched like gravel. The area had the feeling of the outdoors.

After a short time Andreas's staff-sword chinked against a solid surface. I heard a faint click. At the very same moment a light came up—fire light! We had to jump back to avoid being hit by it as it raced through a trough set around the edge of a rotunda. The fire created a wall around the structure. We were on the outside looking through the flames.

The rotunda was encircled by a wide mosaic walk. In the circle of the surrounding walk four black columns supported a mosaic dome ceiling. Beneath the ceiling three wide divans had been cut out of the rock. The divans surrounded a central table also cut from the natural stone. Stone candle sticks topped with black candles surrounded the floor beneath the ceiling. They were unlit. The rotunda was unoccupied.

Andreas worked his elemental magic and an opening formed in the flames. He bowed with a flourish and I stepped through. He followed and the flames became whole again.

I was glad not to be groping about in the dark in a place called Hell. The beating of my heart slowed a bit, but the realization that we could be seen did not allow for diminished fear. The flames that surrounded us gave no cover of shadow.

We avoided the center of the rotunda and stayed as close to the flames as we dared.

On the far side the fire blocked a walkway that joined the rotunda with a wall so high we could not see the top. Three openings were set close together in the wall at the end of the connecting walk. The first was a dark stairway heading up beyond the flames. The next opened to a large room with cushions on the floor and nothing else. No doors led elsewhere. A dim light came from a second stairway. Those stairs led down.

Andreas turned the elements to his will once again and we walked to the top of those stairs with the flame closing once again behind us.

We went down the stairs facing each other, our backs to the walls, and weapons drawn. In the middle of the flight was a wide landing. We crouched there to get a better view of the corridor below. The stairs divided and our view was blocked where a wall separated the two flights.

We moved to the split and crouched again. Both flights opened to an underground crypt, an ossuary, a final resting place of skeletal remains. Most niches we could see were empty, but broken bones littered the floor or remained as refuse in several niches. What purpose was there for a place like this beneath an asylum that leads to Hell? I could only think that it was a place for the dead of the asylum. Not a final resting place at all, but a stop over until the devil had need of another demon. The chill rose up in me again. I didn't need the chill to tell me we were moving toward danger.

With a nod shared between us we continued down the same flight together.

At the bottom of the stairs was a small ante chamber. Beyond that the ossuary spanned out. One row of niches faced us and spanned the width of both flights of stairs. That row was flanked on either side by rows of niches running back into the room perpendicularly.

We stepped out of the ante chamber and we could see the width of the room was filled with row after row of niches with aisles between. We moved down a near aisle and traveled nearly the length of the room. At the end of the rows the rest of the room opened wide to a sepulchral. It was like any chapel dressed out for a funeral, all in black. Black bunting hung just below the ceiling. Black candles in black stone candelabras lined the walls and lit the room in a disorienting haze.

Two exits presented themselves to our left and right, but our paths were blocked by the occupants that participated in a dark ritual taking place before our very eyes.

An evil necromancer stood over a stone slab upon which a taut skinned corpse was laid. Four dark spectral knights in gleaming black armor and helms stood guard at the four corners of the chapel. They looked straight ahead and did not move. Several deformed demons faced the slab. They wore the robes of religious aspirants. The necromancer spoke in low somber tones in a language neither of us knew. The aspirants chanted, much like the chants we had heard from the temple on the pier. This was not a place for the dead, but it was a place for the raising of them.

We pulled back. "There is something about that language," Andreas whispered, "but I can't place it."

The voice of the necromancer rose and spoke in our language. "Do you think we would not know when our house is invaded? There is no place for you to hide here. You are not invited, but I know why you have come. I even know who you are."

We continued to retreat, but our way was suddenly blocked by two of the knights appearing at the end of the aisle. We stopped, waiting for them to come, but they did not advance.

The necromancer continued to speak to us. His tone softened and he urged us to go to him. Our options were bad or worse, and difficult to measure. When we did not comply with the necromancer's urging, the knights began to advance. When they were half way to us two more appeared at the other end of the aisle. Andreas sent a blast of force against those closest to us. They staggered back, but laughed as they advanced on us again. Andreas tried again, this time with fire. They walked right through. He followed with cold and still they advanced.

Realizing he would have to fight, in close quarters, Andreas broke his staff-sword down into two swords. We stood back to back and waited for the assault.

As they approached a strong urge to flee surged in me. I fought it back, there was no place to run.

The first attack came from those who had come up behind and had moved in on us. Then the other two were upon us as well. They fought with great swords and our weapons could not reach them. They hacked down at us as if we were wood for chopping. All we could do was defend ourselves. There was no advantage to be gained against their weapons in close quarters, and they were relentless. We leaned against each other to stay up. Our cuts were few but we were wholly battered. We were beaten to our knees with our swords above our heads, but even that would fail as the strength went out of our arms. My mind raced for a solution, but the fear of defeat muddled my brain. I began to pray for death over capture. Insanity induced by torture at the hands of demons scared me more than death.

"Enough." The voice of the necromancer resonated over the clash of swords.

The knights retreated to the ends of the aisle.

The necromancer came to stand over us; floated to us. His face was gaunt and his eyes shone like a dog's caught in the light. "I can let you live. All you must do is to declare you allegiance to our Lord Devil and I will spare you and bring you to him. I will bring you to him either way, but it will be better for you if you belong to him first."

"Never going to happen," Andreas said.

The master of our fate pointed a boney finger at me.

"What say you, *Saeede*?" He said my name in a drawn out whisper that sent goose bumps up my arms and down my spine.

"How?" tripped off my tongue. I could not manage the rest.

"How do I know your name? You really aren't very bright are you? Do you think we have forgotten how you locked us in? How you killed your own father—a Prince of Darkness? You committed Patricide. You do not deserve to live, but Devil has ordered that you should live."

I had to know once and for all; "Who is Lord Devil? What is his interest in us?"

"Devil is our king. He has no interest in your man whore. It is you he wants; as a gift to a prince."

"What could a prince of Hell want with a mortal?"

"You are so naive. I will leave that for you to contemplate. Your man whore, Andreas, feels brave. He has the scent of godliness, but you do not. Will you come at last to take your place among us?"

"The answer is still, Never."

"Oh, that is an unfortunate reply, my dear. Kill him!"

A great sword sang through the air and sank through Andreas's back and out his side. The look of shock was the last expression he had. My entire spirit collapsed as if the blade had pierced me too. I dropped my blades and grabbed him to stop his fall forward. Blood came up in his mouth and he went limp.

"Take her." The voice of the priest seemed distant. Four arms grabbed me from behind.

"Noooo!!" I screamed, flailing about in the strong arms, attempting to get to Andreas.

Andreas spun on his knees and leaned against the ossuary. He watched with that unchanging shocked look as they took me away. He fell forward, skimming the wall. The tip of the blade struck the ground and jammed there. Andreas fell down the length of the blade and he died. The knight who had thrown it came forward to reclaim his sword and then joined in beside those who carried me. He wiped Andreas's blood from his sword across my face.

The necromancer followed and bent down to meet my eyes. "You should have come willingly, Saeede." Some power of control came behind the utterance of my name. It was the last thing I remembered before waking up, chained by hands, feet, and neck to the floor.

·~·Chapter Seven·~·

I opened my eyes to near darkness. I was lying on my side on a cold stone floor in nothing but my tunic. My hands, feet, and neck were shackled and joined by one main chain that began at the ring around my neck The main chain was short and attached to a thick ring in the floor. There was no lock. The chains, shackles, and floor loop were made of the same glassy black Bane Metal as the gates and fence around the asylum. To an ordinary person the pain that went with the death of their spirit would have rendered them insane. The blood of my father spared me that, but the strength of the chains was unmatched by anything known to Man.

I was alone in one cell of many, in an otherwise empty dungeon, constructed of smooth black stone. Black bars spanned the width of the outer wall. The whole space did not exceed forty fotmals all around. The shape was square. There was not straw for a bed, no pail of water to quench my thirst, no blanket; no comfort at all.

My wounds had not been cleaned or bandaged. My hair was stringy from the sweat of battle and stuck in the blood that covered me.

I could see a white light outside of my cell. It was obscured by the walls of the adjoining cell. I managed to sit, but the chain pulled my head down, forcing me to hunch over. The position was uncomfortable. I returned to the equally awkward but less painful position of lying on my side.

I listened for a long time. No voices came to me. No sounds that I could relate to the shuffling feet of a bored guard. No movement of chains, no groans, or voices from adjacent cells.

I wondered why the chill was not raging through me. It was always a dull presence I had learned to control, but in times of danger it often rose up unbidden. It remained a dull presence.

"Hello?" I said and the quiver of fear and sorrow in my voice surprised me. No answer came. "Hello?" I said a bit louder. Nothing but an echo. I tried once more even louder, but still only the echo in response. The light in the hall flickered, but no sound came to my ears.

My immediate concerns were replaced by excruciating sorrow. I had only just allowed myself to love Andreas and now he was gone. The impact of the loss and the physical pain it caused was unknown to me. My head felt as if it would burst and my chest twisted as if someone actually had a hand around my heart. Tears filled my eyes and wet my face joined by the snot of my nose. I was wracked with sobs and though I tried I could not keep them silent. I curled my chained limbs up tight and hugged myself, thinking that would help, but it did not. My wails echoed back at me. I was ashamed, and yet I did not care. *"Let them hear,"* I thought to myself. *"They will only laugh at what they have done, but when they are sick of me, they will come. The sooner my death comes, the better."*

They did not come. At some point I cried myself to sleep. I don't know how long I slept, but when I woke I was in complete darkness. The white light had been extinguished.

My mourning was just beginning I knew, but the hours that I had cried for him did nothing to relieve my sorrow.

I took up what little slack there was in my chains and began to work them in a twisting motion around the loop in the floor. Back and forth until I bled from beneath the shackle bands. I struggled to sit and felt around the loop for signs of progress. I felt dust, but that was all around me. When they lit the light I would look again. In the meantime, with nothing else to do, I continued my attempts to wiggle the loop free.

Time dragged and I rested many times in my efforts to free myself. Each time I checked my progress with the sense of touch, I felt a fine dust. It was so fine that I could not determine if there was an accumulation or if I was just rubbing over the dust on the floor. The self inflicted wounds on my wrists seared with pain each time I dragged the chain around the loop, but I was obsessed with my task. I was desperate and anguished. My body ached from battle wounds, muscle soreness from my current position, and grief. My frustration came again in the form of tears.

"Dammit, you are better than this," I said aloud. My voice carried and an echo repeated my words for me.

"Get a hold of yourself," I said.

When the echo came back I said, "I'll try."

Time dragged.

I sang our entire repertoire to pass the time. When we performed at court functions we could fill two hours of time if we sang and did not interlude with musical melodies. Two hours; I could tell the passing of time in that way. I could not be sure how long I had been there already, but I was thirsty and hungry.

No one came. Four more courses of the repertoire and still no one. My hunger nagged at me. All the while I worked at the loop on the floor.

When I heard the jangle of keys in a lock, then a creak as a door opened I thought it was a trick of my mind, until the light was lit. There was some scuffling and the rattle of chains, then another creak and the jangle in the lock. I knew in what direction my exit lay. I sat still and waited, but no one approached me.

I looked to where I had worked so hard at the loop. I was saddened by the sight. I had made a bit of dust from the loop, but at that rate I would be dead before I broke through it. My hands and ankles were a sticky, bloody mess. Blood trickled from the band around my neck too.

"Oh, Andy, what were we thinking?"

I flopped onto my side to think of options for my survival, but none came. My only hope was that they would come for me and I could gain some advantage. The Necromancer had promised he would bring me to his Lord Devil, yet he did not come for me.

I slept again on that cold hard floor. When I woke I felt the pinch of a sore throat. Still no one had been to bring food or water. Two renditions of the repertoire and still I was left alone. My throat became tight and swallowing was difficult. I ran the melodies and lyrics twice more through my head and still I was left alone. I became feverish, a welcome condition, at first because it alleviated the dull presence of the chill. Then it went higher and I shivered uncontrollably on the cold floor. I fell into a wild sleep. Nightmares that I could not escape haunted me. A hand came out of the dark and took my hands.

I woke with a jump, intending to defend, but the chains yanked me back.

I shook my head to clear my dream and found that I was not alone. A dark form stood just out of reach, Then I heard a familiar voice—the necromancer. "You need not fear us," he said.

"Why do you injure yourself? You can not escape from this cell."

There was something in the way he spoke to me that made my head spin. The fever was still in me and my throat felt as if it was ripping each time I swallowed.

"Water, please," I croaked.

"It is here," he said. A stone bowl slid across the floor and stopped near my head. I struggled to get to my knees. I would have lapped it up like a dog if I could have reached it. I turned my head to look back at my keeper.

"You are not ready," he said and let himself out of the cell. He shut the gate hard. I could feel it vibrate through the stone floor and the dull clang of the metal gate echoed. I heard the rattle of chains, the creak of the door open and close, and then the keys in the lock. When he went the white light went out. I never heard the footfalls of the necromancer.

The bastard wanted me to suffer. Apparently I had not yet suffered enough. I tried to reach the bowl, but it was soon obvious that I wouldn't be able to. I let out a low frustrated growl and the water rippled within the bowl.

The growl; could I call upon it to defeat the necromancer? Was frustration the key to calling up its power; anger perhaps? Could I do it without the chill that had been subdued by a raging fever. It had not come up in me at Andreas's death. That had been so sudden. I was so overwhelmed by intense sorrow. That was quickly replaced by fear when they captured me. Then the necromancer's voice caused me to swoon and it was too late.

I sat up as well as my constraints allowed. I reached within myself to find the cursed chill beneath the fever. The fever and the chill were opposed and I failed at first to bring the chill to the front. Hours passed before I was able to gain the advantage over the fever. It should not have been difficult; I was so familiar with the chill. I convulsed from the effort, until the chill came more into my control.

When I had control I called up a roar. The gates throughout the dungeon rattled. Perhaps I could use it as a force, like Andreas did when he controlled the elements. Could I put enough force behind it to burst my chains or the doors? Could I conquer the necromancer with it? I doubted that. Still, it was an advantage I did not have earlier.

I tested the roar. I could rattle the doors of the cells but could not gather enough force to break the locks. It was too much for me in my weakening state. I succumbed to the fever and slept again.

When I woke there was a plate of gruel next to the water bowl and the light shone down the hall. I hadn't heard anyone enter the cell or put the bowl down.

That was a concern. I considered why they hadn't killed me yet. They were succeeding at weakening me, though I still had my spirit. Perhaps they were waiting for Lord Devil to have at me. Some devil if he had to have me weakened before he would face me. Phah! devils—why couldn't they leave mankind alone? Why wouldn't they leave me alone?

I was facing retribution for my previous actions somewhere else, on another level of Hell. Necromancer didn't mind reminding me of my father's death, a death delivered by me. They should have be happy. We let some of their kind loose on Earth in the process. Many people died because of that.

I worked on the loop in the floor while I had light, and managed a few growls focused on the glass-like metal. Perhaps I needed to concentrate on a smaller area. The wounds on my raw wrists reopened, and I felt the blood hot from fever. No, the blood was too hot even for that. It was the growl. It was heating the metal! I increased my focus on the growl and metal, but I burned myself badly. The metal would not bend under the small amount of heat I could conjure up.

Conjure –ha! There is a word I never thought I'd use in reference to myself. I shouldn't have used it then; my efforts were so pitiful. Andreas though if he had been there... ."Andy."

Fear, anger, and grief merged in me all at once.

The next roar came unbidden and boundless. The shackles on my wrists and ankles held fast but the chains were broken in several spots. The collar on my neck shattered. Cubes of crystalline metal rained down throughout my cell. Cell doors throughout the dungeon clattered against their locks. Mine popped and the door swung out.

I did not waste a moment. I reached for the water and drank it down, though it had a taste like sulfur. The gruel was awful and I spat it out. I gathered up the remnants of the chain and held them like whips in each hand. They didn't have much reach but they would have to do. I was dizzy from fever and the drain of energy the growl caused, but I had to get out.

The light in the hall still glowed, but no one came to stop me. I moved carefully, but I could not avoid cutting my feet on the metal shards. The room spun and I fell against the wall. I leaned there a moment until I could make out the exact direction of the light. I listened for the sounds of approach. I had just made a terrible noise, certainly someone would be coming to investigate. I knew of only one door. I moved into the hall between my cell and the large square cell in the center of the area. I could see the light shining from a small room off to the side. In that room stood the door that was my exit. The blood of my feet would give me away no matter where I went. I stopped only long enough to rip strips from my tunic and tie them to my feet.

I moved along the bars of the center cell to get a better view into the lit room. What I saw changed me in that moment. In the center of the room hanging from chains in the ceiling was a creature, no—a being. A being of light. The angel?

The being was slender and very tall, having neither the characteristics of male or female. It was badly beaten and barely breathing. There was a commotion and shouting from somewhere outside that door. I went to the creature and stood close so that I could see into the eyes of the slumped head. When I came close a feeling of intimacy came over me. I was not surprised. From all the stories I had ever heard; angels had the power to comfort fears. "I'm going to get you out of here," I whispered.

The eyes became sad, desperate eyes. There was no strength in them. The voice was a dry whisper, but in that moment I decided the creature was female.

"There is no time. You can not break these chains. They are of stronger stuff, even than yours."

The next moment I heard the keys in the lock. I hid behind the door and hoped they would not look there before going to check on me. My hope held.

I had only to slip around the door and be away from there.

"Go," she whispered. "Climb. So that we may live."

Climb? I did not understand. I opened my mouth, I wanted to say, 'I cannot leave you to them.'

"You must." she said.

We heard the sounds of the necromancer returning. "So that I may live. Go." She said, and I obeyed.

The hall beyond was clear. I looked for a way to go and chose quickly. In one direction the hall turned too soon for my liking. I had a hunch it would head toward the population. The other way the hall was straight and long. The further I could get from that room the better I would feel.

I turned toward the population. It was the shorter distance. The long way left me nowhere to hide from the necromancer when he exited the prison.

I was barely out of the doorway and gaining speed when I heard the necromancer. "How?" he screamed. I heard a harsh slap and knew he hit the angel.

My heart raged. I swore I would find a way to come back for her even if I had to command my own Breen Army to do it.

I made the turn at the first corner. I looked about for signs of pursuit and to choose another route. I was relieved to see that my bandaged feet gave no tell to my passage—yet.

Several routes presented. The necromancer was at the door and checking the hall. I drew back quickly before he could spy me and ran again. I was suddenly aware of the chink of my chains. I stopped and gathered them into my hands and hugged my arms in tight. It was an awkward position for running and it slowed me down, but I had no choice.

The first hall I came to had too many doors, too many chances for encounter. The second went down. I had no intention of taking this folly any deeper into Hell without weapons and provisions. The third way was familiar.

The ossuary chapel was empty and the ossuary itself offered plenty of places to hide if I was pursued there. I did not hesitate. I turned into the aisle that Andreas and I had traversed together. I stopped at the dark stains on the floor and wall where Andreas had been killed. How long ago had that been? I had no way of knowing. It was days at least, perhaps even weeks. I bent and touched the stains upon the wall. My grief nearly struck me down, the pain was so physical. I never knew it could be that way with grief.

"Oh Sweet Andy, what have we done? What will they do to you?" For a moment I did not care if I was heard and found. Everything was wrong now. Breen was wrong. Mam and Mya and continuing were wrong. Saving myself was wrong. Finding Andreas and bringing him out with me was all that was right at that moment.

"Sade?"

A distant whisper. Was it possible that he was with me even now? Our love transcended his death.

"Sade." His voice came again.

"Andy. Dear Heart I hear you. Help me, Love. I am pursued by the necromancer."

"Climb. Climb and you will live," he said.

Almost the same thing the angel had said. I heard footfalls coming into the room. I climbed to the highest niche and hid behind a body there.

The necromancer's minions began a search of every niche. One peered over the one in which I lay. He could not get a full view as he clung to the edge. He reached awkwardly and I rolled as far back as I could with my back to the wall and held my breath. He groped the space between me and the corpse, then satisfied that nothing live was there he moved on.

I did not move or breathe for a very long time after that. When I did it was in short little sighs. I was so afraid they would hear me breathe that it was all I would allow myself.

The time stretched into hours, but at last they gave up the search and moved on. They went up to the rotunda and I was trapped. I was forced to wait for the sounds of their return. While it was quiet the whisper of my name came again. "Sade?" This time it seemed so close, so familiar that the loss of it caused a great loneliness in me. "Promise me no matter what you will be strong."

"I don't know that I can." I whispered back to heaven.

"Sade?"

"Yes?"

"Do you know who lies beside you?"

I propped myself up slowly and looked at my camouflage of death for the first time. It was Andreas. His eyes were sunken and his skin was taut. The reality of his death hit me again just as if it had just happened. Then the eyes rolled over to look at me. I drew back and hit my head on the top of the niche.

"Let him alone you demon." I said in my most venomous whisper. Then I leaped on his throat.

"No Sade, It's me I promise."

I loosened my grip but did not retreat. I looked into his bulging eyes and he shrugged. It was that disarming smile that brought me to realize the truth.

"How?"

"The miracle I like to call circumstance."

"I thought I was talking to you in Heaven."

"I know, but I couldn't have you scream or start choking me while they were searching for you."

"Can you move?"

"With difficulty.

"Shh, they are coming back." I lay back down next to him with my head upon his chest. The heart that beat there reassured me that this was my man and not a creature to trick me and take me back to Hell. The necromancer passed by two aisles away. We waited again as they searched the ossuary once more before moving back into the halls. I heard the necromancer barking orders and then announce he was going to report to Lord Devil.

"We have to get out of here, now."

"Grab the carpetbag. It's by my feet. You go first and then help me down."

·~·Chapter Eight·~·

We made our way in the aftermath of the necromancer's search. We were terribly afraid. Demons and minor devils were all around us. Andreas leaned on me. Our pace was extreme for him but he would not let me slow. His whispered prayers for protection came to my ears. I found myself joining.

"God, if you will hear me... ." It gave some comfort to think that some high power could keep us safe from a swarm of evil. After all I had just experienced I could no longer turn my back on the possibility. "...work your miracle of circumstance one more time. Help me get Andy to safety."

In the rotunda the wall of fire was up. Demons climbed and perched upon the stone work. We watched until all eyes were away, then Andreas opened a way through for us. We stepped onto the floor of the rotunda and Andreas put up a small wall of fire of his own. It moved with us and kept us concealed from the demons. The effort weakened him and he sagged against me, but he held the elemental illusion. We hurried around the inside of the firewall to the edge where the dark wilderness began. We were not approached. Andreas gave his last bit of energy to create another opening, then fell. I dragged him through, just as a demon stuck his head around a pillar to look in our direction.

The opening closed and I fell from the exertion of dragging Andreas. He landed on me and we sat catching our breath. I watched the firewall expecting that demon to poke his head through and discover us—he did not. What trick of light that demon thought he saw was dismissed from his mind by the improbability of one weak mortal prisoner walking through fire. He did not know that weak prisoner had stolen from them a most powerful elementalist.

I crawled out from under Andreas and got him to his feet. "Can you carry the bag, while I carry you?" He reached out his hand, but said nothing. I placed the handles of the bag in his hand and then draped him over my shoulders so that I could carry his weight and not drag him upon the ground. I knew I could not open the gate through which we had entered, alone, so I veered away from it. I was certain that the power of the necromancer would be able to tell we had used the magic of the music in that location. Experience told me that an intelligent commander would have an ambush waiting at our point of entry.

Once we were away from the firewall we were in the dark again. This time it was welcome cover. I moved slowly without a staff or sword to feel the way. I stumbled often and ran into several standing rocks, but I managed to keep my feet under me. We were again in wide open spaces. I sang softly through the repertoire then, promising myself I'd stop when it was through. Two hours of time away from that place felt like a safe distance.

I felt the Earth rise and the last hour was uphill. With Andreas on my back it was grueling. As we climbed I could make out a faint light over the rise. That heartened me and I reached inside for my last ounce of strength. I pushed on beyond the two hours of repertoire, but still we did not make the top.

At last, illness and exhaustion would not allow me to go further. We collapsed together. I fell forward and Andreas rolled from my back. Andreas was out cold beside me, but he was breathing. I could not keep the sleep from my weakened, feverish body to watch over him.

I cannot say how long we were there on that dark hillside with the light just out of our reach. I can say that my awakening was one that I had in nightmares. So much so that it took me a moment to realize I was not caught up in a dream, but I was actually living a nightmare.

A giant insect stood above me. I will call it a spider as there were several similarities, but I had never seen a creature such as that before. Six short legs, thin for the total mass of the body, supported it above me. Two more legs probed me, to sense if I was edible or not. The body had two defined segments that I could make out from my position beneath it but it was protected by a hard exoskeleton. I could also see in that flash of time before I screamed that the upper body was a hard round shell like a tick or even like a turtle. All around the edges of that shell fine feather like appendages twitched like the horns of a bat for 'seeing' in the dark.

The scream finally came as I realized the thing was not a dream. I tried to scamper out from beneath it but it matched my moves and I was trapped. I kicked at it hoping to propel it away, but it was heavy and remained above me. The probing legs came down and wrapped around me. Then just as quickly dropped me when Andreas shoved the thing and flipped it off of me. It landed on its back and flailed its short legs. They were not long enough to right it.

Andreas pulled his mandolin from the bag and beat the beast until the neck of the mandolin snapped. Then he used that to stab at the head. It was the only soft spot he could find. I watched in stunned silence. It is frightening to watch the man you love kill a beast from nightmare, armed with nothing but a broken mandolin.

When he was satisfied that the thing was dead Andreas crawled back to where I sat upon the hill. "Are you alright? Did it bite you?"

"No."

"No you aren't alright? Or, no it didn't bite you?"

"Yes."

"Well since you aren't making sense, I'll take it that you are alright."

I glared at him. "Shut up."

He smiled and shrugged.

We sat staring at the dead spider. Andreas broke the brief silence. "Do you think it is edible?"

"What? No."

"We have very little food left. I ate what I could to stay alive."

"Just how did you manage cheating Death anyway?"

"Well, I thought I was dead. I couldn't make my body say or do anything. When they took you away, my heart nearly burst from the pain that caused. I passed out when they drew the sword from me. Sometime later I woke to two of the spectral knights going through the carpetbag. They took all of our spare weapons and the odd pieces of armor you always say you may need someday and put them in a pile. Then they hoisted me up into that niche. The bag didn't hold anything else of interest to them so they threw that in after me. I waited for them to go then I felt around in the bag for the unguent. We had three jars left. I slathered half of one jar on what I could reach of the wounds, front and back, then I ate the rest. Awful stuff by the way, I wouldn't recommend it, but it kept me alive. After that I applied some and took a swallow each time I was awake until I used it up.

"How is it that you managed to avoid death and escaped?"

I told him my story. It ended with: "We have to go back."

·~·Chapter Nine·~·

We sat on the slope of a great mountain and ate a meal of bread crumbs and hard cheese. The silence was palpable as we contemplated what we had been through and what we could do about saving an angel and ourselves.

I found a pair of britches and slid them on. My feet were cut and bruised from our escape bumping around the dark. My bandages were in tatters. One of my dresses torn into strips became fresh bandages and a serviceable, albeit, ragged pair of boots tied together with more strips.

Andreas watched as I wrapped the cloth around my feet and calves. After a long silence he spoke, "How do you expect to go back. We have nothing but my armor, and as I'm sure you've noticed; it has been sundered. Those boots though, they will get you through anything."

"I don't know, Andy. I just know we can't leave an angel in a place like that."

"Are you sure it was an angel? Maybe it was an image sent by the necromancer."

"No, Andy; even that creep, Jest at the edge of Koman City described her to us. Didn't the ledger say anything about angels?"

"Only that he thought The Eye might be nothing more than a falling star. If it was a gift from God he thought it might have been delivered to Earth by an angel. He didn't think angels walked the earth, he wrote nothing like that."

"I don't remember reading that."

"I didn't think it was important. Eindal didn't give angels much attention. I didn't transcribe it."

I was suddenly very angry. "You call yourself a believer and you disregarded that? Don't you think that was information I should have had?"

"I believe in God. I guess I made a mistake."

"What about all that talk about synchronicity? Didn't it occur to you to mention Eindal's thoughts about angels when they were coming out of the woodwork?"

"I just always thought of angels as peoples' misinterpretation of Him. I thought the synchronicity was like a compass point leading us to the Iris. As for the information, I really just thought it was God's hand, working in mysterious ways as they say."

I was quiet for a long time. We were in a very bad way. Having Andreas picking and choosing what I should know aggravated my already irritable mood. I could think of no good way to advance my want to save the angel and retrieve the Iris. We didn't even know what the Iris was, or where. We didn't know where we were for that matter. Hell was a place more vast than we had imagined. I wasn't even sure if we were on Earth or the material plane any more. The gates were like extra dimensional portals.

I kept wondering what the angel meant when she said, "*Climb*". Then, speaking of synchronicity; there was Andreas saying climb when I thought he too was an angel. When I climbed I just coincidentally ended up in his niche of the ossuary. Now we sat on the low incline of a very steep, very high mountain. I couldn't help but wonder if this was more synchronicity.

"I am beginning to believe that there *is* more at play here than just Hell and devils, necromancers, and angels." I said.

"Like what?"

"Like God. I think he wants His things back."

86

"And you propose we go back weaponless and without armor and take them away from Lord Devil?"

"No. I propose we climb this mountain and get a look around. Maybe something will present itself."

"Couldn't we just go back to Koman and re-equip."

"With what for money?"

"I had a bit sewn into that concealed bottom of the bag. The demons missed it when they went through it. It is enough for a few pieces of armor and a weapon or two."

"What about food and water."

"You may have to steal that."

"Why me?"

"Because you are better at it, and because your dark heart will let you put it out of your mind faster."

"Oh, ha ha. You are forgetting that we have no way through the gate. No instruments of the musical or lock picking sort."

"Yes, well then, I suggest we climb this mountain and get a look around."

I let out an exasperated sigh.

We ate a bit more from our broken and depleted food supply but reserved what little water we had for the climb up the mountain.

I was feeling weak from the sickness I caught caged in Lord Devil's dungeon and Andreas was still healing from the ghastly wound he had received from the necromancer's henchman. We hid among the rocks often to rest. It took us three days to make the climb to a shelf that nearly surrounded the wide peak. Clouds surrounded the peak and concealed the sky.

What we saw spread out below us was diabolically beautiful. Three distinctly different landscapes lay below us. One was the red desert where we had first arrived in Hell, the border of that scape blended smoothly into the rolling flat topped hill scape. I could just make out the twinkling lake in the kettle valley. Sharp spires of blue stone shot up like broken shards of glass and bordered the caverns from which we had just escaped. That dark land spread out from there and met the mountain on which we stood.

The last trisection was of multi-colored hot springs and bizarre formations in the midst of a bubbling sulfurous lake. The formations were lined with bright yellow ripples of minerals that floated upon the lake of ooze. We could see no signs of life, but I did not dismiss that something could be lurking in that muck.

Three scenes; three levels of the legendary nine levels of Hell laid out below us. We were at the top of the mountain and to our knowledge had not passed through anymore levels of Hel.l Perhaps there was a central way down to all of the hells through the mountain. That was not our concern though, at that time. We wanted out. We were at the top of the mountain. We must have been very close to Earth firma.

We rested and ate what food we could spare; sipping our water to conserve as much as we could. Then, exhausted, we slept.

No harm came to us on that mountain and when we woke we went straight to the task of climbing up onto the stone shelf and into the mountain caverns and out on to Earth.

We could not have been more mistaken in our judgments. We came through the caverns into a land of stark trees and bramble bushes against a deep purple sky. Low lying fog swept across the ground. We felt cold fingers of it wrap around our legs and ankles, but each time we struggled to free ourselves the fingers withdrew. Only to tease at our hands and throats. We thrashed at them but they were relentless.

My breath caught and my heart pounded in my chest. I had been there before, only then I thought it was another dimension, or at least a dream. It was the place and time where I had been out of phase from Andreas and the paladins. What powers could fool an intelligent mind so completely—or, were we being fooled now?

The mountain continued out of sight into the dark sky above us.

"I have been here before," I told Andreas. "I fought my way back from this shadow realm, stumbling head long through this grasping fog. The trees tore at me. I spun away from one to avoid a gash to my eye. I fell and when I landed I found myself back on the landing with you and the Paladins. I should say, more accurately that I found myself back on the landing observing myself in your arms, with the paladins gathered around us— her, them. I didn't know which of me was dead or alive—which of me was reality and which was dream. You could not see me, but I helped you to open the gate there."

"I knew I felt you." Andreas whispered. "I swore to the paladins that I did."

"I know."

"This is good news though," he said you should be able to find the place of your father. From there I should be able to get us home. We should come out of the prison, south of Mareese."

I looked about me but I could discern no landmarks. I shut my eyes and reluctantly called upon the chill. It had been so strong in me on that first venture into Hell, perhaps it could help me to recall. A sense came over me. As if I stood on some familiar spot and looked toward home. I had no better direction than that.

"I think I can find the way, but the angel told me to climb. The mountain continues. I feel like our way lies there."

"Who am I to argue with angels. I regret my lack of interpretation on that in the transcription of Eindal's ledger. Perhaps we would have gotten a better start on this whole thing if I had."

"You were never one to overlook clues in the past. What made you do it this time?"

"I don't know. As I said I have long thought of angels as a misinterpreted visit from God. I used that as my premise when I went through those entries in the ledger. I wish I had the original with us now. I keep faith with God, He will overlook my error and see us through."

"I wish I could believe that."

"He must be merciful."

"Why must He?"

"Else we'd both be dead by now."

"Sometimes I think death would have been merciful."

"You need to have faith that God is watching over your life."

"Faith? Ha."

"You must have faith in something."

"I have faith in you, Andreas."

"And I you, but beyond that what do you hang your eternity on?"

"I don't know. Life seems just so—chaotic. I assume death will be more of the same or just death—the end,"

"I don't believe that nature is an accident; some result of a chaotic event. There is too much order to nature. To not believe in the presence of God suggests that order can come of chaos. It takes as much faith for you to believe that is possible, as it takes for me to believe in one all powerful god."

"I can accept gods as a race, but one superior being with the power to create all that we know and see—I can't seem to get behind that."

"Even after you saw and spoke to an angel?"

"Even then. I acknowledge that there are things that defy explanation."

"Like why you feel compelled to keep climbing?"

"Yes. When I know we could find our way out of here. It is a mystery to me that I would want to go another unknown way."

"They say God works in mysterious ways."

"Well, if He is working through me that *is* a mystery for the ages."

"No argument here."

"Another mystery is why I put up with you."

He smiled and leaned down to kiss me. "You can't resist me."

"More and more mysteries."

He shrugged, winked, and gave me that disarming smile. "Well, lets be on with it then," he said and started up the steep incline. I carried the bag this time and followed.

We stopped about half way up after pushing ourselves to our limits. My make shift boots were in tatters again and my feet were tender. They needed tending before I could go further. We found a small cave below a hanging rock and went in. There was no sign of animals. In fact there had been no sign of life anywhere along the mountain. It was unnerving, but we took some comfort in that and made ourselves at home.

"We will be out of food soon. The water is nearly gone too." I said, after taking inventory of the carpet bag.

Andreas did not respond. His mind was occupied elsewhere.

I broke off a piece of hard cheese and tore off some smoked meat for each of us. "Suck on the meat, it will last longer."

He looked at me as if he hadn't heard me and reached for the offered food.

"Why does she want you to climb?"

"So that she may live, she said."

"Nothing more?"

"Perhaps if there had been more time."

"We have nothing to go on here. We came for an orb and found an angel. What do those two things have in common?"

I thought I knew the answer immediately, but I mulled it over in my mind. Finding no other apparent response I answered. "Eindal."

He made a dubious face but accepted that possibility. He thought on it a moment longer and then said, "God."

I made a dubious face but it was hard not to accept that possibility based on recent events.

"This is no ordinary mystery. I was approaching it like a theft, but this is no ordinary theft, and now we have an angel-napping," Andreas said. "There isn't one clue, the only crime scene is a battle field back on Koman that we have never seen."

"We have the angel." I offered.

"No, the necromancer has the angel."

We sat back and contemplated our situation. We both heaved frustrated sighs.

"If we could find where the angel was nabbed maybe then we could find the orb. If she had it in her possession that would answer the question as to why God would have let something so powerful out of his control." I said.

"But why send an angel alone into Hell?"

"She wasn't alone. She fell during the battle."

"God must have a reason, or He would have stopped it."

"We should have questioned Jest more. Maybe he could have told us something more about the angel and the one that carried her."

"Neither of us trusted him."

"Yes, but Eindal did at some point."

"I think we are forgetting something. Correct me if I'm wrong, but didn't he say that Evil had won that day; that in the spoils of battle lay the angel? He never mentions the orb, until we ask him about it.

"Eindal thought the orb was delivered to earth by an angel. Delivered to who, where, and when? An orb that shone with a most beautiful azure blue aura. Was it delivered at all, or was it taken from that battlefield? I don't think Jest is telling us all that he knows."

"I've had a bad feeling about him from the moment we met him."

"A chilling-bad feelimg?"

"A little bit, yes."

"Jest never mentioned the orb to us. He told us only of the angel's capture."

"There were a lot of angels, and a battle. It is possible he never saw the orb that day."

"We need to know more about his meeting with Eindal."

"Why would he tell Eindal about the orb and not the angel? Why tell us about the angel and not the orb? Are they both the truth, and he has chosen only to tell half to each of us."

"If that theory is right then what are his intents?"

Frustrated sighs and then silence. I did not tell Andreas that I had deeper suspicions of Jest. I wondered if he could be Lily. Andreas slept with his back against the cave wall. I ran over the last weeks' events in my mind. The whirl of contradictions just gave me a headache. I did sleep eventually. But my mind was no more clear on it after sleep.

We sipped water for breakfast and then climbed.

We climbed long and hard. Our lack of nourishment made us weak, but we had to push on. We climbed up and up. We rested and climbed again, up and up until we looked over three landscapes spread out beneath a black sky.

We climbed a little further and even through that black sky, until we came onto a ledge that brought us up through a cave to three more landscapes.

The mountain still rose above us. The sky was covered with a soft veil of clouds high in the sky that foretold of wet weather . The clouds gathered at the mountain peak, hiding it from our eyes.

We stood in a stone forest of high and wide grey stone. The magnificent, landscape created countless labyrinths. I would have trouble walking there in my bandaged feet. The stone was close together and sharp toothed animals climbed all about the stones and hissed at us if we came close.

We did not tarry there and moved up the mountain until we could see the three separate landscapes.

"That makes nine." I said as we continued up toward the clouds.

"Should we try our theory about being close to Earth now?"

"That was my intent."

"Last one is a demon spawn." Andreas declared and shot passed me.

"I may as well take my time then." I called after him, and I did.

He waited for me just below the ring of clouds.

"Remind you of anything?" He asked when I was in earshot.

"No flying until we know what is on the other side."

"Alright," he said with feigned disappointment.

We rested and drank the last of our water. If Earth was not on the other side of those clouds then we had little hope for survival.

We climbed through clouds for a very long time. Sometimes they were so thick that we could not see each other. When that happened we whistled or sang to keep ourselves together. When at last we came out of the clouds we found ourselves at the opening to a vast cavern. The ring of clouds hung just below us. We entered the cavern and wound through a network of caves until we came out and land spread out before us. I looked above us and the mountain still went on, up and up into a familiar sky. Two familiar moons were rising while two suns hung above the eastern horizon.

How we passed through the land I do not know, but I wasn't about to climb back down to find out.

"Earth?" Andreas whispered next to me.

"Or a trick of the devil? The mountain still climbs."

"Looks like a city there." He pointed and I followed his finger. Blue smoke rose from the chimneys of a cluster of buildings spread out along a narrow river.

"Maybe we can resupply."

"I'm for that." I said, "but remain vigilant."

"Aye."

·~·Chapter Ten·~·

We walked down off the mountain and wound through standing stone and gnarled trees. At the edge of the trees we turned onto a worn wagon trail and approached the city. The air was thick and smelled of fly ash, something we had become familiar with during our time with the smithies in Breen. Everything was covered in a black dust. The main commerce of the city was in metal and metal goods.

A lopsided sign at the edge of the city read Pyritia. A flash of chill went through me and I held Andreas back with my arm across his waist.

"Does the name Pyritia mean anything to you?" I asked.

He thought then answered, "Something Father Gan said once, after we opened Scroll Dominus."

"Yes, of course. There is a Hell Gate here. In the slums I think." I turned to look back at the mountain It just looked like a mountain with the summit lost in the clouds.

"What are you thinking?" Andreas asked.

"I don't know what to think. So much of this seems impossible, surreal."

"Yes. I guess we can't let that stop us now."

Andreas bowed and swept his arm in the gesture of a gentleman allowing a lady to pass. He is so confused sometimes.

I moved ahead and he trotted up beside me to take my arm. People stopped to watch us as we passed. We knew right away why. Although our shabby clothes and tired gait matched theirs, our coloring was pale compared to the bluish cast of their skin. Sometimes they were so blue as to seem black. I remembered the words of Jest at the edge of Koman City and wondered if these very human looking people could actually be another form of demon. They did not attack us, but that only alleviated my fears a little bit.

We found a blacksmith a few blocks in, but his specialty was not armor and weapons. He directed us as he looked us up and down. We left his place and made our way to the indicated shop.

The shop we were directed to was a good recommendation. The smithy was a master and we found all sorts of weapons and armor, much of it in styles we had never seen before. He was expensive and we could not replace all that we had but I came away with two wide silver scimitars, two long poniards, a bow with two scores of arrows in a quiver, as well as a breast plate. Andreas outfitted himself similarly but paid extra to have his two silver swords attached to a short metal stave. We waited until the work was done and asked about a bootery and general store. He gave his directions and gladly sent us on our way. Pyritia did not suffer strangers gladly.

We spent the rest of our coins on boots for me, a set of thin files to serve as lock picks, and food enough for a week if we rationed carefully. We followed the river upstream and left the city. We filled our water skins on the river bank beside a thick copse of trees. The trees were good cover and we made an excellent camp. I went on the hunt for edible meat while Andreas gathered wood and built a fire. I grew more confident that we were actually back on Earth when the wildlife was what I was used to. I shot two rabbits cleanly. We would eat well and I didn't lose an arrow. We cut the leftovers into strips and smoked it in an oven we made of stone from the river.

We spent the rest of the day discussing our next move. It was key to solving our dilemma that we talk to Jest in Koman City. We stayed the night in our camp. The next morning we ventured back into Pyritia only long enough to inquire about how to get to Koman.

"Ask the wharf master down river."

It was all we got and all we needed.

Late that night we came to the mouth of the river. It fed into a large gulf of warm water. Three buildings stood at the river's mouth on the opposite bank. A bridge spanned the river a little way up from the gulf. What the man in Pyritia had called a wharf was no more than one wide pier and no seaworthy vessels were tied there. No buildings were lit so we slept along the shore.

We woke to the sounds of a small dandy pulling into the pier. One man jumped out and tied down. We had no way to pay for passage, but we were willing to work for it. We got up and ran to approach the man before he could enter a building.

"Excuse me, Sir," Andreas called to him. The man looked about and stopped when he saw us. We slowed to a walk and closed the distance.

"Sorry to bother you," Andreas began. "My wife and I are in great need of passage. We have been set upon by all sorts of villains and spent the last of our funds outfitting ourselves after they nearly killed me and took all that we had. My wife only narrowly escaped their capture. We are minstrels and the few instruments we have left are broken. We can not play for you but, we can work it off if you will agree to take us to Koman."

"Koman?" He laughed. "Not with my dandy. I've only pulled in for a game of bones with a friend. If you can wait I'll take you as far as Howeleigh."

"On Ahzdahn?" We asked as one.

"You know it?"

"I grew up there," I was saying as Andreas was saying, "She grew up there."

"I don't remember you." The man said giving me a closer a look.

"I was sent away in my youth. I became a minstrel. That life took me away for a long time. I haven't been back for years."

"Who are your parents?"

I had hoped he wouldn't ask. "I didn't know my father. My mother is Pria. She was a midwife there. She left shortly after she sent me away."

"Well I don't know her either." He looked us over again and then said. "Well, I said I'd take you. No charge, I have to go back anyway. So unless something better comes along I guess I'm it."

We didn't want to wait but there was nothing we could do about it.

"We'll be here." Andreas said. "Unless something better comes up."

The man nodded and continued to a building where he let himself in.

"Let's go check out his boat," Andreas said.

We walked down the pier to see that the boat was well maintained.

"I think something better just came up," Andreas said. I looked out to the gulf, but there were no other ships.

When I looked back Andreas had untied the dandy from the pier locks and was raising the mizzen sail.

"Don't just stand there. Get in and man the tiller."

I couldn't find a good argument to stop him so I jumped in and did as I was told. After the mizzen was up Andreas worked the elements and a good breeze pushed us away from the pier. I turned the tiller and we backed out as if we knew what we were doing. I didn't know where Pyritia was in relation to Ahzdahn but I knew Koman had to be north so I turned us north. The sails filled with the natural breeze and Andreas raised the foresail. We were well away from the pier when the man and his friend came running and yelling down the pier. The friend had bow and arrows but he didn't have the distance.

Fine thing that the King and Queen of Breen were now pirates.

Andreas came to take the tiller. "North west will get us to the coast of Ahnges. It will be open sea, but I don't see any weather on the horizon," he announced. I went through the carpetbag and found a cracked vial of mother's seasick remedy. I ran my finger along the glass to get what I could of the remaining liquid. It would have to be enough.

"I can't believe we just did that." I said.

"Exhilarating wasn't it?"

"No. I feel awful. We left that man stranded."

"We needed to go. We can't wait around for some mopes to play bones. We have an angel to save. We will make it right later."

"How? We don't even know his name."

"Oh, well I didn't think of that. I don't know, but we can figure that out when the time is right."

"Thanks for dragging our names even deeper through the dirt of Howeleigh." Frustrated sighs were getting to be a habit. I let an exaggerated one loose and slumped back with my arms crossed over my chest.

***

Eight days later we were working the fishermen's wharf in Sandhitch so we could buy food. Six days more and we came along side the Night's Angel. Captain Knight was flummoxed but relieved to see us.

"You wouldn't believe it if we told you. Just leave it at things didn't go well. We are back for another try at it. We need you to take us ashore. We can use the dandy but don't let anything happen to it. We are just borrowing it."

Captain and crew were nice enough to only ask after our welfare and leave the story for later. We were soon back in Koman City and looking for Jest. He wasn't hard to find. He had a ramshackle place built of scrap and drift wood in the alley he had tried to get us into on our first meeting.

We found a place in the shadows and watched the little house. Other people lived in the alley too. We were shooed from our spot. A place in the recess of a boarded window. It was home to an old man. We did not argue, but he spit at us as we left. Further away but still in view of Jest's home we found a place between two dwellings of similar construction as Jest's. We sat against the wall facing Jest's hovel and watched. I set the carpetbag beside me, on the side away from the main alley and we snuggled together beneath Andreas's cloak. We looked like any of the other homeless sprawled about in similar niches.

No one came or went from the little hovel. We waited all day and into the night. When all was quiet and the moons had passed overhead we walked to the door.

So, he had gotten us there anyway. I knocked on the short door while Andreas knocked on the overhang of the low roof. A quick scuffle of activity took place inside and Jest put his face up to a grimy window.

"Lor, Lor," We heard him say and then he was at the door. He opened it a crack and sized us up. When he was sure of who we were he opened and motioned us in while he looked apprehensively up and down the alley. "Still alive. Ooowe! What brings you here to me?"

"We have discovered a possible link between your story and our purpose here. We want to know more and we can pay you." Andreas said.

"I'm list'nin.'"

"Well we need to know about that creature of light you described."

"How much do you know?" I asked.

"How much you payin'?"

"For all of it; something to live on now, passage off this hell hole, and gainful employ when we get to our final destination. The amount depends on the value of your story," Andreas said.

I hadn't told Andreas about my suspicion that Jest could be Lily. He would have become too hostile and I was afraid that would cripple us even more. I didn't want to pay Lily. I wanted to kill her, but if I was wrong and this was just a poor man then I had to be careful and went along with the plan Andreas set up.

He seemed excited until the words gainful employ came out of Andreas's mouth. "What kind-a employ?"

"We were thinking fisherman. You can refuse it if you don't want it. You will still be off of Koman. We can drop you anywhere between here and the Islands of Bekua if you prefer."

Jest rubbed his chin and began to pace.

"Come on Jest," I said. "We are offering exactly what you want and need. We are in a hurry."

He thought a moment longer and then agreed.

"Tell us everything you know about that creature, beginning from when you first saw her." I demanded, relieved and excited that it had not taken more to convince him.

"I saw her a few times, before the demon had her. She seemed to be looking for someone or something. She would come close to town, hiding in the rocks and looking over the city from one end to the next, up the streets and down. I tried to get close, but she always seemed to know when I was near. Just when I thought she'd be around the next rock, she wouldn't be there when I got there."

"When did you first start seeing her?" Andreas asked.

"Let me see. It's comin' on summer now. Goin' on three years, little more mayhap."

"Did Eindal ever mention her to you?"

"No."

"He never said anything about angels or The Eye of God or anything similar to that?" I wondered. I was playing a dangerous game. If this was Lily and she didn't know about the orb I was peaking her curiosity. I looked around the room as she spoke. I didn't see any wigs or false noses. There was no closet. I saw no chest or anything large enough to hide a varied wardrobe for various characters. There were no feminine touches at all.

"He was more likely to mention Hell Gates, but once he said somethin'; like he was trying to figure in his head—somethin' about God's hands being guided by God's eyes"

This time I watched the person in front of me. "So you never saw him with an orb?"

"No."

He wasn't nervous, although I could see he didn't trust us. I remembered Lily had been much taller When I first faced Lily as herself I had seen the guardsman she had portrayed in her eyes. Jest was shifty and his eyes darted about, but his eyes were grey, and older. Lily's had been a clear blue. My suspicions subsided, but I couldn't take my eyes off of him.

"What about the angels. Did any of them carry any kind of standard, a scepter or orb? Maybe one wore a jeweled crown, anything that could have been a setting for an orb?" Andreas wanted to know.

Jest thought about that, but shook his head no and said, "Nothin' that I saw."

"What about the army of bright creatures? When did you first notice them?" I asked.

"They came in twos and threes, so if you weren't payin' attention you'd never knows they was there."

"Didn't people in town get nervous when strange creatures walked amongst them?"

"They were never in town, only in the mountains."

"Were they all looking for something there?" Andreas asked.

"No, just the one. The others were preparing for battle."

"How did the battle start?"

"Like I told ya, all sorts of devils and demons came up when some idiots fooled with the gates. Eindal was on a quest to stop them but he didn't have all that he needed and came here looking for answers. He didn't know then that there were already gates opening. Up there in that asylum there must be a gate. Maybe it was what the bright one looked for. The devils came just like the angels; one, two, three at a time. They found the bright ones there and sent for more Hellions to join them. When they had the numbers they swarmed over the rocks and engaged the bright ones in battle. The bright soldiers fought against the dark devils. Many fell on both sides.

One dark devil with black feathered wings commanded the dark army from his place 'tween the asylum and his army. The bright army tried to drive them back, but there was too many of the dark army and the bright armies suffered many more losses before they fled.

The dark army searched for the spoils left on the battlefield. When the leader found something the dark army swarmed around him. They made quite a commotion. When he emerged from the center of the gathering he had with him a soldier of the bright army. I

105

think it was an angel; it was so full of light. It didn't have wings, but it was tall, very tall like the winged demon. They bound it all up in black chains.

"Where did you see the demon take her?"

"I saw the demon walkin' through the mountain, like he was going home to the asylum."

"Could you take us to the places where you witnessed this?"

Jest thought a moment, he was nervous, and regarded us with a wary eye, but then nodded affirmatively.

"How soon?"

"It's comin' on daylight. I could takes ya now."

An hour later we stood in the spot where Jest hid as he watched the angels gather. He laid out the scene and the sequence of events for us once more. Next he led us to where he had first seen the devils gathering closer to the asylum. Andreas and I made an extensive search of the paths, but we found nothing.

He took us to the battlefield and the spot where the demon had found the fallen angel. Nearby a tumbled pile of rocks was spilled across the trampled ground. That was not odd since Jest's story told of a commotion around the spot where the angel laid. What was odd was the one set of clawed foot prints visible over the trampled ground. This could only have happened after the devils had taken the angel back to the asylum. What had they returned for? My money was on the orb, lost in the battle.

I kicked at the stones and overturned a flat shard. Something was scratched into it. I bent to pick it up and saw a roughly drawn map, and two words that shocked me—Come Sade.

I was so overwhelmed that I swayed and had to lean against the rock.

"What is it?" Andreas asked.

I placed the shard in his hands. Andreas shook his head in disbelieve and I stared down at the map in his hands. It was easily recognizable. The mountain—that never ending surreal mountain.

"Climb, so that we may live." I said.

"Huh?" Jest responded.

"I thought we would find the orb here." I said, no longer caring what Jest heard.

"It's addressed to you."

"I see that. How?"

Andreas shrugged. "Not many people call you Sade."

"Only those closest to me."

"Who would know you by that name and know you were coming here?"

We stared at each other trying to use the empathy we had nurtured over the years to help us see what was hidden from us.

I turned to Jest. "Did the demon ever stand on this spot?"

"I don't think so. The angel fell over there." Jest pointed. "It crawled here where the demons captured it." He pointed to the trampled ground.

I walked to where the angel had fallen. I could see that blood had soaked the earth. There were no corpses left to examine. Even devils and demons remove the dead, but for very different reasons. Dirt and pebbles were churned up around the spot where the melee had taken place. A few hand prints of a large human, most likely the angel's moved away toward the spot of capture. The prints disappeared; untraceable in the trample of battle. Any other clues were obliterated.

I walked the sixty or so fotmals to where she had been captured. "The angel fell in battle here? She was wounded and made it here from the main battle?" I asked again.

Jest raised an eyebrow at my mention of gender, but he made no comment. I did not pursue it, hoping he would forget my slip of the tongue. We had not wanted him to know that I had actually seen her myself.

"This way." Jest moved through the mountains with the grace that only comes from familiarity in such terrain. We followed as quickly as we could.

A sudden feeling of dread came over me and I wanted Jest gone so Andreas and I could analyze the area privately, "Can you get home okay on your own, Jest?"

"Been doin' it fer years."

Andreas reached into our carpetbag and took out the lantern and oil that Captain Nights had given us as a signal. Then he emptied five silver coins into his hand and gave them to Jest.

"Here is something to live on for now. I want you to get what you will need to be comfortable on a sea voyage. Use this lantern to signal our ship off shore. They will send some one for you. Lift and lower the hood; two long lights followed by a short and another long. Tell him we will meet them in Mareese and Breen will have to wait. Andreas did not tell him that we had worked that message out with our captain just in case it was needed. Any other message and Lio Nihoc would know Jest to be a liar and had our permission to toss him overboard.

"Things may not be safe here for awhile. You should go as quickly as possible. Our captain will see to your employment if you still want it. If you leave him in Mareese you will be watched until the authorities there know whether or not you can be trusted."

"I can be trusted," indignant Jest said. "You are a mistrusting pair."

"We have reason to be, but we aren't so bad once you get to know us," I said. "If you ever have that opportunity. Now get going."

Jest put the coins in a pocket, took the lantern and oil, and disappeared into the mountains.

When we were sure he had gone we moved close together and looked down at the map. In the center was a quick outline of the mountain surrounded by three sectors. I recognized the kettle lake and the bridge. One quadrant was plain, except for a small square. It had to be the red desert and the black pedestal. Had I not already seen the three quadrants from the mountain I don't think I would have recognized the third. The hot springs were indicated by groups of three wavy vertical lines to show the geysers. Contouring lines were drawn within the mountain. Each smaller than the next to indicate elevation. Between the last contour and the next to last were the letters S-A-D-E.

"Looks like you have been expected." Andreas whispered.

"Yeah," I breathed.

"So do we climb, or go after her?"

"She has been here so long already. I wonder if she is even still alive after my escape. The necromancer blamed her for that.

"Still; *'Climb, so that we may live.'* And now this... ," I said and flicked the map with a finger.

"We did climb. We escaped and now we are back. We had to climb to accomplish that. Maybe she knows our reputation and figured we would come back for her," Andreas reasoned.

"That still does not explain my name on this map at about the same time that we were moving on the gates nearly three years ago."

"Perhaps God had taken an interest in our activity then. The angels were here to fight back the escaping demons because we could not be in two places at once. An angel fell as they retreated and was captured."

"Maybe, but why keep her prisoner for all those years? There must be something that Hell expects to gain from that."

"Or perhaps the angel still expects to gain something for Heaven."

I shook my head, disbelieving. "You have such faith in all things heavenly. I wish I did. Still, I have begun to believe; in angels at least."

"I don't understand any of this. I wish we had never gone to Behlanna, I wish we'd never heard of Eindal, or scrolls, or any of this."

"There is an angel being held prisoner, and from what I saw she is being tortured; that I know. What I don't know is; to what end? Let's go get her. If she is still alive she can likely explain the rest."

"I'm with you. Let's go."

Andreas placed the little stone map in a pocket of his breeches and we set out to find our way back to the asylum gate.

***

I knew the cams of the gate lock and they turned smoothly with the help of the files we purchased in Pyritia. The gate opened without a whisper of noise. The oil we had used on the hinges our last time there had seeped in nicely. We slipped into the yard and I pushed the gate closed and relocked it. We padded swiftly up the stairs and landings that led between the wings of the mansion. I drew my two new scimitars and Andreas held the bag close with one arm, and carried his staff-swords in the other hand.

We had not checked for traps when we entered that first time. We thought then, that the occupants would not expect anyone to go willingly into so menacing a place. There had been no tricks or traps to harm us then. This time I checked. We were afraid that they might expect our return. The time was wasted, there were no traps.

At the door I listened. I could hear the now familiar sounds of distant moaning, sobbing, insane laughter, and the drone from the portal pedestal deep below the building.

I looked at Andreas. He was ready and gave me a nod.

Not wanting to let our guard down, I checked the door for traps again, but found none. The door was locked, but easily undone. We slipped into the opulent vestibule and shut the door behind us.

At the opening into the foyer I ventured a look around. Someone was on the stairs, but they were moving away from us. I watched as they turned a corner and went out of sight. A door opened and closed, but the horrid sounds that came from that room sent chills down my already chilled spine.

From the foyer we looked into the library. Two dark figures in priestly robes were seated at the table and bent over a large tome. They sat side by side and faced us. If we caught their attention I didn't hold much hope for our success. We moved one at a time across the opening, taking one large step to the other side. Andreas peeked around the opening, and the priests still had their heads into the book. We saw no one else about, but we could hear noise from the kitchen. We walked to the closet as if we belonged there. No one called out or tried to stop us.

We climbed into the small elevator and I lowered us slowly to the basement. We unloaded and returned the elevator to its start position. We shared a quick look and joined hands as we stepped onto the spot in the floor that we knew would take us to one of the deepest levels in Hell.

·~·Chapter Eleven·~·

We turned in the direction of the red sky fading to blue and ran towards the flat topped hills. It was not long before the sand rose up and fell away to reveal a horde of doppelgängers. They leaped toward us but we were expecting them and surged passed them toward the hills. They gave chase. More and more rose to join them as we closed on the hills. Breathless and spent we turned to meet them. I stood before Andreas brandishing my scimitars with all the skill I could muster. The front line hesitated at my display while Andreas gathered the heat from the desert sands. Then confident in their numbers they came at us.

Andreas landed a blast of fire in the center of them. The flames caught easily on their oily skin. A mass of them fell and died writhing in the flames. The flames licked easily to those nearby in search of more fuel. Those stumbled through the surrounding ring and fell to the ground to extinguish the flames. Several more caught as the others stumbled by.

Those that advanced on us and threatened to surround us were heedless of the flaming deaths behind them. Perhaps they could not actually hear the screams or smell the acrid smoke of the dead.

Andreas prepared another blast. I felt his elemental power build and timed two deftly placed blows on two doppelgängers just as he placed the next blast directly behind those in front of me. Two more fell, dead and burning. Several others broke and ran leaving us with seven. Andreas stopped and blew out his breath, then inhaled slowly. The sand behind the doppelgängers swirled up and engulfed them. I backed away while Andreas lifted them and thrust them back across the sands.

We were left alone then. We hurried on.

When we looked over the edge of the hills at the village built up on the lake in the kettle valley it looked like any other busy fishing village. The denizens were not cloistered away in their temple this time. If it were not for the hunched gait of the creatures we might have wandered in looking for a meal at a lake side inn. Instead, we knew the reality of what they really were.

We had only narrowly escaped two of them the last time we were there. Our attackers had become food for the great fish that lurked in the lake. There was no doubt that we would die if we faced the whole village. We needed a way around.

Settling on the best of our bad plans we made our way through the hills to the far side of the lake. When we were above the entrance into the hill, we jumped. If we missed the pier that connected the village to the catacombs then we would have to climb the pile posts and pull ourselves up onto the pier before the great fish could eat us. If we were successful and hit the pier—a broken limb or two didn't seem out of the question.

We waited for the bridge to be clear of traffic. Then we jumped together with Andreas propelling himself further away from the hill so that we would land in line with each other but not impede each other as we landed.

Like acrobats we dove feet first, then tucked just before impact, and rolled to absorb the shock. But, we were not properly prepared for the speed and the erratic trajectories our rolls would take. The edge of the pier came up quickly and Andreas could not stop his bulk from going over and splashing into the brackish water.

I let go of the carpetbag and caught an arm around the top of a pile post. I managed to keep my upper half out of the water, but strained to pull the rest of me back up onto the pier.

I ran to where Andreas had gone in and saw him swimming for the surface with the great fish close behind. I lay down on the pier and reached an arm out to him. He surfaced and caught my arm. In one desperate motion I rolled as I pulled and our combined momentum got him clear just as the fish took a bite of the pier. We scrambled for the solid footing of the cave entrance with the force of the impact rocking the pier. I lunged back out just in time to keep the carpetbag from slipping into the water.

We ran through the familiar halls to the shaft filled with the swirling mephitic gas. Without hesitation we went quickly down the surrounding stairs to the landing and stood before the gate.

I braced myself for the soul wrenching shock I knew would come from the blood red metal. Without our instruments I had to endure it physically to manipulate the massive lock. I got us through, slammed the gate shut, and locked it as quickly as I could. The task sapped my strength. Andreas carried me away from the gate. He sat me on the ground and then sat himself next to me.

I knew the look I leveled at him alarmed him. My head hung low and my mouth was agape as I looked out from under my brows. He pulled me to him and held me tight. He spoke comfort in soft tones and rocked me until I regained my strength.

There we were again in that utter darkness. We held each other in the quiet; gathering strength and courage for a very long time. Time was against us, but I was incapacitated. We could not afford to push on until I was well enough to continue. When I was, we made our way in the direction of the rotunda.

The gravel soon changed to solid stone and we heard the faint click we were hoping to avoid. We jumped back at once as the fire raced to surround the rotunda floor.

The fire wall lit the area and we could see the imps still perched all around the rotunda. Man-like but with reptilian skin and leathery wings, they lounged on the stone benches and table, or clung to pillars, or hung from the roof by their long gnarled feet. All heads turned toward us. A cacophony of chilling laughter filled the air and they advanced on us, slow and catlike. They came through the fire unscathed. Their faces full of malice.

I dropped the carpetbag and drew my scimitars. Andreas snatched his staff swords from the clip at his shoulder and spun it before himself. We avoided many fights in the past just by demonstrating our weapons skills. These creatures were not impressed. They stopped only long enough to hiss and move on us again.

They came to my waist. I could fight them with some difficulty, but their stature made it hard to defend against them. Andreas had better results using his staff.

I just kept my stance low, bending at the knees to meet them more-or-less eye to eye.

They snarled, clawed, and flew at us with gnashing teeth. We fought long and it seemed they would never quit coming when Andreas had one of his moments of inventive magic and he spun the staff-sword like a pin wheel on a horizontal plane. He often used the force of the elements around him, but this was propelled by the force of momentum and he had control of that. He drew a poniard and defended with that when necessary, but he had the staff sword moving in a lethal arc before us. What I did not cut down, the staff sword did.

Andreas spun the staff sword up and then down and back to his hand. His attempt to show off was botched when the staff-sword nearly snapped his wrist, and clanged against my chest plate before he could get control of it.

I gave him my best annoyed look, but I was actually impressed with how his mind worked and what he could do with it.

"Go ahead, take a bow. I know you want to."

He not only bowed but did a little leap before landing on one knee and throwing back his head with his arms flung wide and the staff-sword spinning just out of his reach.

I shook my head. "The great and powerful Grandiose!" I said. "Can you do anything else?"

He waggled his eyebrows. I tossed him the carpetbag, put a sword in each of my hands, and moved toward the wall of fire. When I turned away I was smiling. He was kind of magical—to me at least.

"What, not spicy enough for you?"

"Not right now," I said. "You want to get us through this fire wall?"

He opened a way and we walked along the wide mosaic corridor that circled the rotunda. When we came across from the stairway down, Andreas worked his elemental magic and an opening formed in the flames there. We passed through and the flames renewed behind us. We stood once more at the top of the stairs that led to the ossuary, and beyond that, my prison, and the angel.

We went down facing each other, our backs to the walls, and weapons drawn. At the split in the stairs we crouched in the landing for a better view of the room below.

We could make out the niches and the litter of broken bones, but we saw no one or nothing else in our line of sight. We listened and waited. We did not hear the incants of the necromancer and no one moved passed our field of vision. If we were to complete this complicated mission to save the angel and solve the mystery of the missing orb than we could stall no longer. We knew that once we stepped off those stairs we would be at full offensive. With a nod shared between us we continued forward.

As we stepped out of the ante chamber at the bottom of the stairs we caught a flash of steel in our peripheral vision. We spun and got our weapons up in time to meet the attack of two spectral knights who had been hidden in alcoves to either side of the stairs. Sparks flew at the impact.

The sheer bulk of the knight was nearly enough to take me down, but my small size against his great height made me difficult for him to target. We were not confined between the rows of ossuary There was room to move in the area outside the burial niches. Adopting the tactics of the imps upstairs I darted and spun, jumped and rolled about, slashing and jabbing at every opportunity. Even I was impressed at what I could do. I landed stabs to the gut from under my arms with my opponent behind me and spun with one weapon held across my chest and the other at my back, slashing deep into the knight's unprotected thigh.

As impressed as I was with myself the knight remained unharmed even from my silver blades. I was beginning to panic and wondered if the undead could actually be killed. Then a time came when he bent to run me through. I rolled and his blade rang against the stone floor. I rolled back against his blade and my weight disarmed him. I looked up at him and saw an exposed area beneath his fauld. I drove one scimitar and the then the next up under the ribs and into the spine.

One sudden spasm and the Knight slumped; paralyzed. I rolled out from under him just in time and sprang up to aid Andreas. When he saw me he moved to turn the knight away from me. I never liked to attack a man from behind, but these were not men. Evil had to be taken down in any way that we could. I moved forward and with alternating swings of my blades I cut the knight in twain.

We stayed long enough to take pauldrons and greaves from their armor to enhance our own. Their great swords were too much for me to wield and Andreas preferred his staff-sword so we took up both knights and their weapons and stuffed them into a high ossuary niche.

We moved down the aisle then, and into the sepulchral. The black candles in black stone candelabras lit the room in a sooty haze. I had not had time to notice on our first foray that the flames in the candles were a small black flare. Even the light in the place felt heavy—evil. I felt the chill in me increase. Fear rose up, but I fought the urge to run. I wanted away from that place of black magic, of death, and necromancy.

No one was in the sepulchral or in the halls but I felt as if we were watched. No, I knew we were watched, the feeling was familiar. Something—from my father.

My father. *"Impossible,"* I told myself. I shook off the feeling as a trick of the surroundings. Just as the place had played on my fears and attacked me with apparitions on the day I found my mother in some other part of Hell. We moved into the hall and I thought no more of it than that.

We could hear sounds from corridors and behind closed doors. I am reluctant to call them sounds of everyday life, but that is as it seemed. Mute voices and laughter, the lilt of a haunting melody, the clink of glasses, and a distant door creaking open and then shut. Often, the sound of advancing footfalls caused us to stop and wait. Once we came in earshot of a conversation and stopped until it ended and the participants moved off. To say that we were on edge would be an understatement. Every sound might be one that led to us being discovered. With great care and trepidation we made our way to the prison door unhindered.

A smear of blood swiped along the wall on one side and then stopped. We each placed an ear against the door to listen. A nod from Andreas told me that he also heard nothing. I checked the door, it was unlocked.

Once inside we shut the door behind us and shut out the torchlight from the corridor. Andreas obliged with one from our supplies. It guttered, but caught and revealed an empty prison. No angel hung from chains, no cell housed a prisoner. No one was present.

Andreas looked to me for an answer, but I had none. The room was clear of all but a row of shelves along two walls. The third wall was empty except the door from which we had entered. There was no fourth wall; where it would have been was open to the center cells and the walkway that surrounded them.

119

In the center of the ceiling, a round lever backed hook was driven into the ceiling and secured by a metal bar. Three thick rings of chain were suspended from that hook.

We searched the room and the surrounding cells for clues to the angel's fate.

Below the hook the floor was coated with blood. Old, black blood was the largest and bottom layer. On top of that was a newer layer of brown, and then another at the center, just below the hook. The top layer was a glossy, rusty brown patch. It can take days for blood to dry in the damp conditions like those of the underground cells. The fact that the top blood layer was not completely dried, meant the angel could have been in that room as recently as four hours earlier. Sadly, that number was generous given the conditions. She could have been gone for as many as fourteen days by our best estimate. We calculated that we had been gone for twenty four.

Several boot prints and one set of bare feet smeared the rust colored blood on the floor and scuffed through the dry layers. Shallow scratches in the wooden door indicated that someone had clung to it with their left hand. A bit of fingernail was caught in a split along the grain. Next to the door we found the beginning of the bloody right hand print. It smeared across the wall and more scratches in that print told of a desperate attempt to cling to that wall. Below that the left hand had grabbed briefly, but the stone gave no hold and the hand was pulled away The right hand print smeared and was dragged along the wall, indicating the direction they had taken her. Bloodied boot prints faded off in the same direction. Her struggle gave us a shred of hope that she could still be alive.

Andreas found an oily spill on the top surface of the shelves, but we could not determine the origin. We weren't about to taste anything in that place. The smell was like the carnivorous flowers in the Jungles of

Bekua; an odd blend of floral aroma and rot. We went on the assumption that it was a drug

All other signs of struggle I could explain as having been a part of my escape.

Back in the hall we examined more of the bloody hand print until her grip was broken and who ever had taken the angel away finally gained full control of her. We knew what direction they had taken. We were relieved that the ossuary lay in the opposite direction. With weapons drawn we went the way the blood led us.

We could not be sure beyond the initial evidence which way they had taken her. Many halls and doors presented options. No further signs of struggle presented us with answers and the blood on the bottom of boots wore off. The sounds of living went on all around us. We heard no cries, no moans of pain, or pleas for mercy. Then we found a drop of blood, then further on another. The trail had not been lost.

A vision came and the chill came with it so hard that I could not move against the cold of it. I recalled that first moment of awe when I had laid eyes upon the angel for the first time. I fell behind Andreas but he didn't notice. I could not hear him. I watched him through the vision as he moved ahead of me.

There was the angel, surrounded by denizens of the dark. They swayed in unison as if they moved to some rhythm. She was suspended a few inches off the floor. Chained by her hands to the ceiling and by her feet to chains in the floor. Her body sagged forward. A black throne flanked by two braziers lit with black flame faced her. In the throne a man sat casually with his feet draped over the arm on one side of the throne. He seemed to be speaking to the angel, but I could not hear the words over the pain in my head.

I collapsed and was next aware of Andreas patting my hands and face and I was slumped against a wall.

"What happened?" he asked.

"I had a vision. It came with the chill. It hurt like hell, but I kept control for a moment and I saw it clearly." Although the world still spun I smiled. "I did it, Andy!"

"Ya, well try to warn me next time will you? You shook with seizure. I didn't know what to do, or what had happened."

"I am sorry. Eble didn't warn me about that. I guess that is what I must go through to make the visions come. The seizure was just me shaking from sheer cold.

"I think I can find her now. At the last moment of the vision I think she felt me. I think I feel her now. She is surrounded by people of this place and a king. If we are to save her we will have a terrible fight to do so."

"Did you feel in your vision that they were about to kill her?"

"No, it was more like they were entertained by her. The king was casual and speaking to her, but I could not hear him. She was slumped forward. I could only see the back of her. I looked over her shoulder at the king."

"Do you think the king is this Lord Devil that you mentioned?"

"I'm sure of it."

"Then let's go to this place. Maybe we can find a place to hide until she is left alone or taken elsewhere, we can diminish the numbers of opposition and increase our odds of saving her."

"That is worth a try," I said and got to my feet.

It was not much of an effort to find our way. We only used the blood trail to confirm my hunches. I could feel the angel. My heart became light. I felt like a child. She came softly to my mind and spirit in a way that made her feel familiar to me. I knew that we had connected and that the angel clung to that connection to bring us to her.

There were no instructions, just a sense of the angel. It was as if she called to me from some far off place and all I had to do was follow her voice, but there was no voice. It was her essence, a life force, or spirit that called to me and I had to keep my mind clear of all else to follow it.

I shuffled along the halls with Andreas close beside me watching for passersby. He reached out and pulled me back three times. Twice the denizens passed by so closely I thought sure they would spy us out, but they were intent on their own tasks and passed by.

The third time we were surprised as we came around a corner and nearly stepped out into a busy plaza. Andreas pushed me back into the corridor and pulled me into the recess of a door as several denizens of the dark passed by the end of the corridor.

Each time we had to avoid contact my thread of connection with the angel faltered and I had to grasp at it quickly. I nearly lost it all together as the vastness of the plaza invaded my thoughts. When I steadied myself and regained the thread I knew that the angel was somewhere in that plaza. I didn't know how we would manage to get through it unseen and unaccosted.

The corridor was like a back alley. Stacks of boxes, sacks, kegs, and odd items of tools lined the walls. While I struggled to keep hold of my connection with the angel, Andreas worked at the door behind us. He hoped to find similar storage inside. His hope paid off and we let ourselves in just as several denizens turned into the corridor. We listened to be sure they passed by, then Andreas locked the door behind us.

"It has been a long day," he whispered. "We will rest here and eat. After a while I'll slip out and check the traffic. These creatures of the dark must need to rest sometime. When they do we will move on."

I nodded agreement, but worried that I would lose my contact with the angel. I put my mind to a difficult task. If I could correlate my sense for the angel with the space of the plaza and our position next to it, then I might be able to get us near her even if I did lose contact. I had no desire to search door to door for her. I had some success and narrowed the location to an area at the approximate center of the plaza. It was good that I had. I was tired and dozed off; losing contact with the angel.

We woke to keys turning in the lock and scrambled to cover among the goods stored in the room. Two very human looking demons came in and found what they came for staged near the door. They loaded heavy boxes onto a small cart parked outside. When they left they locked the door again and we listened as the cart creaked away into the plaza.

Andreas put an ear to the door, then unlocked it and peeked out. He held up a finger signaling me to wait, then he slipped out. The door shut quietly behind him and we were separated. It seemed a long time that he was gone. I strained to listen for him; and became aware that traffic in the plaza had lessened considerably. I realized I would not hear Andreas unless he was discovered and that allowed me to relax. I tried to re-connect with the angel, but I was unable.

Andreas returned and reported that he had found a place where we could watch the plaza and plan our next move together. I told him I could not reach the angel, but that I thought I could get us close to her.

We moved out and locked the door behind us.

The place Andreas found was behind a bench in a corner of a high wall, and a stairway, that led to the top of the wall. A wide walkway with a swirling pattern of mosaic flared out from the bottom stair and decorated the plaza floor. Several rises and falls in elevation broke the flat surface of the plaza. Some were rounded structures that swirled up in great sweeping walkways that went no where and served only to look over the plaza. Other walls jutted up and out and seemed to have no purpose but to break up the space. All around the perimeter walls we could see dark openings; the corridors like the ones we had navigated to get to the plaza.

One oddly shaped building was the focal point of the plaza. Situated slightly off the center of the plaza, the inverted ziggurat raised four floors in stories of ever-increasing size. The building blocks seemed to be of uniform size, but were set randomly on any one of six possible sides, and stacked in no discernible pattern. Many of them jutted out over the plaza while others were pushed back and would have to be jutting out over some portion of the internal structure. Many of the stacked blocks had balconies cut into them. Some on the edge over the plaza, others set back looking down over the blocks set below them. Several gates were set at equal intervals along the outer wall at the plaza level.

I tried once more to reach the angel but failed. I would have to rely on my best guess. We whispered our ideas. I wouldn't call what we had a plan. We moved out on a prayer.

I had a strong feeling that our angel lay somewhere within the building of geometric blocks. We felt as if we were being watched even though we kept well hidden and no one was near. We ran between the jutting walls and swirling walkways, watching each time under cover, before moving to the next.

One last jutting wall blocked our way and we ran to it. Lying on the ground behind it, we peered around the corners to get our best look at the structure. At each gate stood two spectral guards. An aura of evil shrouded them. Scarlet robes covered their field plate armor. Around their waist they wore thick black girdles. Over their robes they wore layered plate pauldrons fashioned to be like a screaming face looking over the shoulder. Horned black helmets gleamed even in the dark surroundings. Visors covered their faces, but a dim glow emanated from the eye slits That spoke of magic—black magic and that was not good for us. They carried long swords and cudgels. The head of each cudgel was a skull. Some were skulls of Man others were of beasts.

If we could manage to approach and deal with one pair of guards without alerting those at the other gates we might be able to survive and gain entrance to the gate. If we did we had no way of knowing how long it would be before the dead guards would be discovered.

We drew back to the protection on the back side of the wall.

"Last chance to back out." Andreas whispered.

I have to admit I thought about it, but I couldn't leave the angel behind any more than I could have left a child. "No." I whispered back.

"Okay then," Andreas replied. He took my hand and held it to his lips. "I am proud of you, you know?"

"Yes, and I am proud of you. I trusted in your faith and we have survived."

"So far. Believing in the just in case seems to pay off too."

"Well, just in case faith isn't enough; do we have a plan? What should I expect from you?"

"I think I can borrow from the darkness and keep us cloaked and silent at least until the fighting begins."

"If you can do that maybe we won't have to fight at all."

"How do you plan to get through the gate?"

"Not the gate; a balcony. We climb."

"That's a lot to concentrate on all at once. I don't know if I can."

"Faith, brother. Keep the faith."

"I admit I like the idea, but if I can't do it... ."

"It doesn't matter. I don't hold much hope for survival either way. I just know we have to try."

"Faith Sister."

We smiled nervously and sat in silence trying to conceive a better plan for avoiding the guards. We could think of nothing else.

Andreas bent light away from us. I kept one hand on his shoulder and the other around a scimitar. I guided him to a spot between two gates. We made it in silence and unseen in our shroud of darkness. One block laid on its side and was only four fotmal high. It was set back from the others beside it and offered us cover.

I laid my scimitar on the ground and made a step for Andreas with my interlaced fingers. He made the top of an adjoining block and I placed my scimitar at his feet, then I climbed as he maintained our concealment. I moved us further back between two blocks and prepared for the next climb. I had to make the climbs easy for Andreas. The next had me on hands and knees as he stepped up on my back and pulled himself up easily. We had to cross that block, drop down and climb another, and then one more on the tallest plane before we were beside the first and lowest balcony in our climb.

At the tallest block there was nothing I could do. Andreas would have to climb too. I squatted with my back to the wall and allowed Andreas to stand on my shoulders. He faced the wall, to keep his balance and I used the wall for support as I raised him so he could reach the top of that tall block. I strained under his weight but completed the task. Our concealment faltered when Andreas strained to pull himself up over the edge of the block. I looked into the plaza, and watched, waiting to be discovered. No one came. We had gone unheard. I jumped to take Andreas's outstretched hand.

The balcony was dark and the room beyond was unlit as well. No doors or windows separated the balcony from the room. It was a simple matter to sit upon the balcony wall and swing our legs over. We stepped aside of tables and chairs at the front of the balcony and entered the open room. It was furnished like a salon complete with a side bar stocked with all types of liquor. I wondered how strong a beverage had to be to intoxicate devils and demons. Andreas must have wondered the same thing. He went straight to the shelves and took down three bottles. He wrapped them carefully in what was left of our clothing and placed them carefully in the carpetbag.

I listened at the door until he made his selections and came to join me. I turned the toggle lock then, and opened the door enough to see that the area beyond was huge. Just outside the door a stone concourse curved with the wall in which the door was set. On the other side of the walk, rows of seats circled an arena.

I saw no one, so I opened the door wide to get a better view of the entire space. The sound of some activity on the floor of the arena came to our ears. We could not make out what the activity was from our position. We had to cross the wide concourse to see over the stepped seating.

I moved first and crawled along the seat backs toward a wide column that supported the ceiling. A rush of wind came at me from the arena floor and in the wind I heard my name. The shock of fear stopped me in my tracks. I knew the voice—my father's voice! The fear of possession gripped me. I fell to the ground and curled up with my hands over my ears to protect me from his voice. I prayed, "Protect me great God. If you have purpose for me here, protect me."

Andreas was beside me whispering comfortingly. He did not know what apparition had come for me but he would protect me if he could.

The chill rose up and the familiarity of it during a time of danger was a comfort. The fear subsided and I crawled to the pillar. Andreas was right beside me and we stood with the pillar between us and whatever was on the arena floor. We stood side by side with our backs to the pillar and ventured a look over our shoulders and around the pillar.

At the far end of the arena was a covered stage. A row of chairs flanked a throne at the back of the stage; facing the arena. The dark handsome king from my vision stood before the throne and looked up toward our position. The orange light of glowing braziers cast a sinister light across his face. The necromancer stood among the shadowy forms of bent and withered, spirits; chanting and gesturing wildly. Suspended from the ceiling of the stage was the angel. A wisp of white rose up from the angel and circled the heads of the man on the stage and the enthralled spirits at his feet. We did not know what foul magic could be at play but we knew it was not good for the angel.

One lone figure jumped down from the stage, crossed the arena, and made his way toward us. Malisgalar, my father. I knew not how, but he was alive, and he was coming for me.

In the brief moment that it took us to see all that was before us I asked God to comfort my mother if I should fall to Lord Devil that day. We drew back against the pillar and looked into each others eyes. There was fear, but determination. Andreas bent to kiss my head and then with a nod we drew weapons and turned to face Malisgalar side by side.

He laughed when he saw us. "Oh my child, you are so like me," he said, and his form changed to a gorgeous auburn colored man. "Do you see how you favor me?"

I did favor him and it angered me. The chill grew.

"Surprised to see me I see. Did you really think that your puny swords would keep me dead? I am a prince here. Only Lord Devil is above me. When it was discovered that I had been murdered they dug me out of the rubble of my tower. Devil's necromancer was sent for. He tended me well and here I am today. I intend to claim you once and for all, or to punish you for my death. Either way should prove satisfying."

He motioned with his arm to indicate the scene below us. "All of this is for you. This is what brought you here. You will be mine when this over. When at last we draw the spirit from the angel beast yours will come more easily. You will be heir to all that is mine, and you will be glad of it."

"We've had this conversation before. The answer is still, never."

"We'll see." Malisgalar turned his attention to Andreas. "I am a bit surprised to see you. It seems you are harder to kill than we thought," he said and took a step toward Andreas. I moved between them. "Oh, I see. So you *do* love him then?"

The question went unanswered as Malisgalar swiped his arm out across his body and flung a mass of power to hit Andreas in the neck and shoulder just above my head. The force of it launched Andreas from his feet and sent him hurtling down the concourse. He landed at last, rolling and sliding into the wall where the concourse turned on its way around the arena. He looked broken and for a moment my heart sank. I could not go to him while we were still threatened. He staggered to his feet and I turned back to face Malisgalar who was about to fling his force at me.

I dove into the seats and the mass of power roared by just above me. I jumped to my feet, leaped back over the seats to the concourse, and ran to where Andreas rested gathering his own strength.

A pillar blocked me from Malisgalar's view. For a moment it was my best protection, but as soon as I was out of cover a mass of force screamed down on me. The chill warned me; becoming even colder. I had an impulse and acted.

I turned and let all of the anger I had ever had for my father build in me. It came quickly; all of it from when I thought he was just a weak human man who had abandoned me. All of it from the times when a father's love could have given me protection and hope, but was absent from me. All of it from the torment he had brought upon my mother, for her desire to abort me after discovering what he was. All of it for the torture he had played out on her to get to me. The chill grew as the emotions rushed up, raw and hard. I nearly went to my knees but I quickly had enough anger in the chill to unleash the growl on the thing that was my father.

It came and when it did it threw me back. I landed on my backside, and watched as the force rolled along the concourse. The seats shook and Malisgalar stood waiting, mocking me as the force bore down on him. When it hit he was rocked back but he kept his feet. The force that was my growl hit the wall behind him and rocked the ceiling and doors as it dissipated.

Malisgalar flung another mass of power and in my position I could not scramble away fast enough. It hit me and a painful deadening of my nerves shook me. I went numb all over. I couldn't breathe and my scimitars flung out of my helpless hands as I ricocheted off the concourse wall and crashed into the seats in the curve of the arena.

I heard cheers and the tremulous deep voice of Lord Devil. "Oh, good move!" he shouted.

Andreas had regained his strength and was there to force me up. Malisgalar was about to unload on us again. Andreas stood between us and raised a force all around us. "Find that chill again, and fast. I have an idea. Let me know when you are ready to let it go."

I did as I was told. "Ready," I said.

"Go!"

The protective shield came down and Andreas called his own elemental powers into the force I had unleashed. I could see it grow in strength and size and it turned like a ball of blue ice as it screamed down on Malisgalar.

This time Malisgalar showed fear in his eyes, but he was confident in his own power and stood fast. His hands came up and some magic came to repel the ball of ice. Even that was not enough as Andreas let it into the thing that would impact Malisgalar in seconds. Sparks roiled and popped within the ice. Andreas began to sag and I put my arms around him to hold him up. The ball hit and Malisgalar was instantly transformed into blue ice. The sparks now roiled and popped within him. He sounded like ice shifting on a frozen lake.

I helped Andreas to sit against the seats, took his staff swords, and ran to where Malisgalar stood still rocking from the impact. Eyes the color of the ice followed me as I came to him, but his body was frozen.

I leapt across the last few fotmals and swung the staff swords over my head with all the strength in my body. The head of Malisgalar flew into the seats and was smashed into smithereens against the backs of seats lower down. His body wobbled back and forth. I pushed it over to break upon the concourse.

Malisgalar, my father, melted on the concourse and in the seats. He would be nevermore. I hated him and what he had done to my mother to make me. I was a demon spawn and I loathed him for that. Many times I had wished I'd never been born and that Mam had killed me in her womb. Why the finality of his death grieved me so then I will never understand. There was no time to consider it at that moment. The angel was near and we had come for her.

·~·Chapter Twelve·~·

The arena below was silent.

Andreas gathered up my scimitars as I stood at the top of the aisle Malisgalar had taken to get to us. I looked down at those in the arena, disbelief gripped the faces of everyone there. Lord Devil had come to the front of the stage. The necromancer had turned his attention to us. The white wisps floated away into the air and were gone.

Andreas joined me and without exchanging weapons we moved down the stairs. The withered, shadowy creatures fell back, until they were against the stage and behind the necromancer.

"Do you have a plan?" I asked Andreas as we closed.

"No, but I think I can turn whatever they throw at us back on them."

"Good, Let's stay together then. I'm going for Lord Devil. We need to get him away from the angel."

"Right."

The necromancer began to incant. Andreas sucked the wind out of his throat. The creature fell in a fit of coughing. We went straight to the stage. The shadowy things that did not move aside fell easily to the staff swords. The others broke and ran up into the seats splashing through the remains of my father. Lord Devil remained calm as we leaped onto the stage.

He backed away from us, but he was up to something. I could see it in his eyes. He mouthed no incant. He made no motion except to continue backing until he was behind the chairs near the back of the stage.

Suddenly out of the braziers beside him a tempest of smoke and cinder formed. It was a complex elemental, but I expected Andreas would have the situation dealt with tidily. I spun the staff swords nimbly in case they were needed, and stepped back to let Andreas have his way with the thing.

He threw back his head and arms to gather the needed elements to him. When he had what he needed he let loose several short bursts of heat into the thing. Steam rose and lightening roiled within the elemental. I expected it to explode in a downfall of rain, but instead the wind gained velocity and it spun faster. Loose stone and dirt along the edges of the walls came to the thing and spun out from it to pelt us. The chairs lifted and were flung at us. It came toward us gaining speed and strength all the while. We were pulled toward it. The air became thin around us. Andreas tried to harness the wind to turn it back on Lord Devil, but Devil borrowed from Andreas and transferred that energy into the vortex.

Sparks showered down on us.

The wooden ceiling began to snap. Shards of wood broke away and joined the great force of the vortex. Some were flung wide. One struck my arm and the pain caused me to release that hand from the staff-swords. The weapon flew away for a moment but the vortex brought it back to spin with the chairs and wood shards. At some time it too would be flung free.

My feet were pulled out from under me and I began to slide across the floor toward the vortex. Andreas bent to grab me, but the strength of Devil's elemental pulled him down and he rolled passed me into the roiling cloud.

I reached out, instinctively grasping at anything to stop my slide. I felt something cold and gripped instantly around it. The pain of the blood red metal—Blood Metal, went to my soul, but I held on by sheer will to survive. I looked to see what it was, to tell if I could get a better hold. Three rings of red chain were in my grasp. They were attached at the bottom to an eye ring bolted through the floor. At the top they were attached to shackle bracelets around the angel's ankles. I looked up and met her eyes. They were dull and I worried for her survival as the wind tossed her about between the chains at her feet and wrists.

The Blood Metal sapped my spirit and I had no good idea how to battle the vortex that had taken Andreas. I thought if I could get to Lord Devil and kill him the vortex would stop. The problem was I had no good idea how to kill Lord Devil. I clung to the chain with both hands, but I was growing weak from its effects. My body whipped about like a pennant in the wind.

Something came to me in those moments. Like a presence, yet my own thoughts. *"It is like anything else you have faced in life. He is using your own turmoils against you. Stand strong against him as you always have. Do not let him use what they made of you against you."*

"How can I stand against this wind?" I said. I did not worry that I was answering aloud to voices in my head.

"It is only a manifestation he created out of your own fear, doubts, and self-loathing. Take it back from him."

I looked up into the angel's eyes. She was telling me to give up my doubts and the wind would die. A chair hit me and I lost my concentration. Was I wrong? I was losing my grip on the chain.

"What?" I shouted.

"Stand strong. You have fought these turmoils all your life. Do so again this one last time and you can beat them forever."

I had dealt with strife all my life; that bred self doubt. Mam and I lived with poverty and persecution. When I returned from my tutelage in martial arts my mother was gone. I feared she had been murdered, but I often wondered if she had abandoned me. I scratched out an existence with my music, but that often wasn't enough. People were reluctant to hire the ragged girl from the streets, so I often stole from those who rejected me.

Before I knew who my father was I already doubted my worth. Evil was in my blood. It was in my parentage. For as long as I could remember I had pushed it back. My mother raised me with goodness. I wanted to be good. I took that into my adult life. I believed it kept evil from over taking my spirit.

Foolish as it was I still felt worthless.

Foolish—the word rolled around in my thoughts. Foolish to let those thoughts define me. Foolish to think I could kill the devil with physical force. This was a battle of mind and spirit; good, ultimately, versus ultimate evil.

I called upon God, the king of good. If the Lord Devil was the king of evil, then I could use the help of the king of good. I felt like a pawn, but a pawn for good at least. "Use me God. Help me to save your angel. Help me."

A calm washed over me. I let go of the chain and the vortex pulled me in. Andreas knelt in the middle with his arms out stretched at his sides to keep the winds at bay. I began to list things in my life that had been touched by evil and recited what I had done to conquer them. I had my doubts about the affect on the vortex, but the winds did eventually begin to die. When they did I felt the devil at work against me. He was proficient at bending my mind to accept the sins against me. I strained to keep my perspective. I could no longer let him mine the darkness that had been in my life. I called on the good in my life and pushed it back at him. The winds lessened again and the debris fell.

Andreas became aware of me. I was in a battle he did not expect of me. He stood and came back to back with me, to protect me from what ever may come from behind. Just being near him renewed my spirit and the vortex dissolved. Lord Devil backed away from us.

"What manner of mortal are you?" He asked.

"The good kind," I said.

That voice of lost memory came to me. *"The medallion,"* the angel said. *"take it so that I may live."*

The devil wore a clear crystal medallion on a gold chain around his neck. I did not hesitate and lunged at him to yank it from his neck. I should have known it would not break. Lord Devil's laugh echoed throughout the arena. I should have let go but I struggled to either break the chain or pull the medallion over his head. Devil's laughter continued, then he grabbed my wrist and pulled me to him. We looked eye to eye. His power was apparent and I became awed of him.

Andreas realized the peril I was in and he surprised the devil with a fist to his chin. Our eye contact was broken. The devil went down from the force of the punch. I went head over heels with him, but I held fast to the medallion. The medallion came with me as Devil hit the ground.

Andreas quickly changed his focus from the devil to the angel. He strained to manipulate the elements to bend the chains that held her suspended between floor and ceiling.

I put the medallion around my neck, then ran to retrieve my scimitars from where they had landed when they were flung free of the vortex. One stuck hard into the back of a spectator seat high up. The other laid on a low stair leading up to the concourse.

The devil got to his feet quickly and bore down on Andreas as he struggled with the chains. I had only obtained the one scimitar from the stairs and was not close enough to way lay the devil. I aimed and hurled the scimitar end over end to hit the devil in the chest. He saw it coming at the last second and he was suddenly in my location. The scimitar spun over Andreas's head and sank into the wall at the back of the stage.

The devil put a hand to my throat. His strength was startling. I could not breathe and my eyes throbbed behind their sockets as he attempted to crush my throat. My ears rang loud. My head seared with pain. My struggle to remove his hand from my throat weakened. I could see him laughing through a swirl of colored lights behind my eyes.

I was losing when the blade of my scimitar pierced through the devil's chest from his back. He dropped me then. I struggled to get air back into my lungs. The devil turned with the blade protruding front and back. He faced Andreas and pushed the blade until he could reach over his shoulder and pull it out. No blood dripped from the blade. He laughed again and teased the blade around in front of Andreas who weaved about to avoid it.

I could only watch as new breath filled my empty lungs. From behind Andreas the eerie voice of the necromancer had rejoined and was incanting. I felt myself being lifted and there was nothing I could do to stop it.

Then I saw the angel. She faltered in flight, still weak from her ordeal. She scooped me out of the sky with one arm and removed the medallion from my neck with the other as we swooped low over the seats.

She landed and placed me gently on the concourse. She steadied herself against a pillar and placed the medallion around her neck. Whatever that medallion was it strengthened her.

She took flight without benefit of wings and swooped down on the necromancer who incanted once again. She grabbed him up in both hands and flung him against the devil who was about to run Andreas through.

The two evil beings, in a tangle of arms, legs, and scimitar slammed into the seats along side the stairs. The necromancer broke under the devil's weight and was no longer a threat, but the devil kicked him away and ran at Andreas with the scimitar before him like a lance.

Andreas looked about for something to arm himself with and settled on a fallen wood shard to fend off the blade. His effort became unnecessary as the angel banked around the rim of the arena to swoop down and pick him up. She cradled him like a baby and pulled her legs up, then forced them down on the devil's shoulders. The force propelled her still higher while knocking the devil down the stairs.

She came to land beside me and set Andreas down. They helped me to my feet and I got my first unrestricted breath.

Lord Devil was on his feet again and raged foul curses at us from the floor of the arena but he did not advance on us.

"We must go," the angel whispered and cradled us each in one arm and heaved her massive legs to lift us high above the plaza. She banked to the left and the arena was quickly behind us. We flew above the flat topped hills that concealed Lord Devil's necropolis. The rotunda fell behind us and we passed over the the kettle lake. She was taking us to the mountain; the core that ran between Hell and Earth.

She landed high up on the lowest tier to set us down gently and then eased her worn body to the ground. She broke the medallion on a rock and breathed in the white light that escaped. Her cloudy eyes cleared. "That is better, but it has been a long ordeal. I must rest before we go on," she said in a soft whisper.

"We will watch over you," I said.

She stretched out to her full height of nearly twelve fotmals. I marveled at how large a creature she was. All the times I had seen her until then she had been slumped in her chains.

She was not what I expected an angel to be. Her skin was not the alabaster from the lessons of priests and storytellers. She was browned from prolonged exposure to the sun. She was not circled with a bright halo, but glowed with a soft light. Her hair would be the color of cinnamon once she cleaned up. Her clothes, like that of a soldier, were torn to bits, except for three bands of gold cloth wrapped about her torso.

Andreas went to hunt for food while I stayed to watch over our new charge. Who had saved who? In the end it was she who got us safely away. I looked upon her with awe in my heart. So many tales of angels.

We even sang a couple of songs about angels in our performances, but I had always considered them mythical. How could I believe in devils all my life and not in angels?

After leaving the persecution of the city my youth had been joyful with my Mam, in our little forest hovel. Still, my thoughts pulled to the dark side of life often. I never let my good Mam see that in me because I loved her and did not want her to know that of me.

Mam never told me what my father was. We were each protecting the other. In the end it had been for nothing. He still tried to destroy her to reclaim me. He did not care if I was destroyed in the process. As I sat looking at the angel I wondered if our not telling had been some control my father had over us.

I loved music with a passion and I had mastered harp and flute at an early age. Why had I also sought the martial arts? Had that been a compulsion manipulated by my father as well, or just a wickedness of him that I inherited? So many doubts had weighed in my life. Now they felt like a cumbersome chain that only answers could break. I hoped the angel could provide them.

Andreas returned from his hunt with a raven. An omen of my past forbade me to eat it. In my woods, as a youth a white raven flew. Mam told me that it was a sign of protection. If that was true then what did a black raven mean? Andreas walked back down the mountain and buried the carcass. We rationed our meager stores and ate lightly.

We let the angel rest until we saw organized legions marching out from the gates. Dark blue, green, purple, and black demon soldiers led by fiery red beasts we had never seen before. The angel was exhausted, but we managed to get her moving at a crawl. We moved around the mountain out of view of the legions and began our climb under cover of the rocky face.

Angel strained but knew she must continue. We assisted all that we could. Andreas pointed out legions approaching from each section.

They came toward the mountain, across the red sands, and over the flattened hills. Legions of reptilian demons slithered or sloshed through the waters of the bizarre hot springs beating and stabbing at tors and hillocks along their way to the mountain.

We pushed on into the next levels. If we could climb widdershins up and around the mountain we would come to the Hell lands of my father. From there Andreas could lead us out and we would be in Crystalier and close to help. I hoped that the people of Mareese would forgive us for bringing Hell upon them again.

***

We flew over the land of my father's realm cradled in the shaking arms of the exhausted angel. Once I got us to the ruins, Andreas called out directions that took us back to the gate that would take us up to the prison and close to home.

At the gate Andreas and I worked together once more to minimize the time either of us would have to touch the Blood Metal. Hours went by and we knew the legions were merging together and advancing on the land of Pyr. We needed rest, but fear fueled our energy and we continued with renewed urgency.

Much had changed in the prison. It was more like the asylum, but here priests and physicians cared for the shattered souls of prisoners who had faced cruel manipulations by the forces of evil. We avoided contact easily and led the angel through the prison to the basement window we had crawled through on our first foray there.

The windows had been sealed with stone blocks and mortar from the inside We took our blades to the sodden mortar and water began to trickle in from the flow that we knew would be just outside. The water helped us to make quick work of the stones. We pushed them out against the incoming flow of water and set them against the outer wall.

When we climbed out Fionaghal and I watched for guards while Andreas turned the elements to his will once more and sealed the stones back into place. With that accomplished, the angel took us up into her shaking arms and took us into the air.

She swooped low to the floor of the gorge then arched her body to climb the western plateau out of the prison gorge. We could hear the exclamations of the soldiers on the prison roof. We rose ever higher. The air grew thin and Andreas and I became sleepy, but I trusted the angel to take us to safety.

I woke on the summit of a snowy mountain. A blanket of thick white clouds blocked my view all around. For a brief sleepy moment I had forgotten that we were safely away from Hell.

The angel lay in a heap beside me and Andreas slept on the other side of her. I watched over them until Andreas woke and we watched over the angel together. We watched with our weapons drawn, expecting dark legions to swarm over the mountain at any moment.

When she woke I offered her food and water and she took them without a word. She took the water in small sips then in large draughts to quench her long thirst.

I asked where we were.

"Far from the mountain of Hell; somewhere outside of Mareese. I do not know where exactly." Her voice was strong; no longer a weak whisper.

I watched her. She seemed forlorn—beaten. We sat in silence as she ate and then she drank the rest of the water. Suddenly something reminded me of why I fought so hard to stay on the right side of humanity. I despised evil, for what it had done to me and Mam. Because of that I felt honor bound to protect good from evil. Here was a creature of goodness and that touched my heart. I suddenly felt as if I knew her. Whatever it was I knew that I loved her.

Finally she spoke again, in my head. I looked at Andreas to see if he heard it too, but he was lamenting our lack of food and water. He was unaware of anything unusual.

She noticed my stare and spoke again in my head to reassure me. All at once I realized—I knew her.

"Do you recognize me, Sade?"

My unspoken thought was acknowledged.

"I am so glad. I am sorry that I lost you in the devil's web. His tricks were working on you and there was a veil between us. You fell into a very dark temper. Then just as I found you again you were gone from me."

She was very excited, but I didn't understand what she was talking about at first. I began to understand when she continued.

"You were mired in Devil's tricks. I lost you even before you went into the old Mage Academy on Duke Mediwen's behalf. I knew the circumstances around you were going badly, as early as that. I could feel the dark ones all around us. They were seeking you and conjured a veil that kept me from you. I tried to get close and battled many of Devil's and Malisgalar's minions in my attempts. I lost an orb in one of those battles. It was a loan from God. My ability to transport myself from place to place in an instant went away with that orb. They kept me busy and events moved so quickly around you that I could not keep up. I could not get to the right place at the right time.

"That old mage academy was a sanctuary for evil that was already seeping through Hell gates, even as Eindal sought a way to stop it. Old Mediwen was a pawn for Malisgalar's minions and it was easy for them to convince him that the academy needed to be eradicated. They knew you were making your way there to perform for him. They acted as peasants and nobles and bent his ear until there you were as is sent by heaven. I tried to reach you then before you entered the old duke's gates but they fought me and I failed you again.

"The veil became stronger and for a time I could not even see you. Then I heard the sounds of battle at the academy and knew you must be there. One of them wore the orb I had lost, around his neck. I went for him but he had knowledge of the power to transport. He vanished and I was overpowered; beaten to unconsciousness. They left me there that way and I lost track of you again.

"I began to spy on Devil's spies in order to find you again. When I did you were walking along a road where you were ambushed. There were more than brigands on the road that day. Devil's minions were all around you. I fought as many as I could to keep them off of you, but I was nearly captured then, and you still had need of me. I would have been no good to you captured. I retreated, but drew many away from you when I did.

"When Eindal was murdered any doubts I had that your father was at play, were eliminated. Eindal was known to me and I knew that he often sought holy relics. He wanted to protect the relics of good and destroy those of evil if he could.

"I watched helplessly as events unfolded. I recognized that you two must have been involved, but still I could not get through to you. If I could have I would have given aid."

I was speechless.

She continued to explain, "When the paladins came to assist your quest they prayed well and the veil became tattered. It is in that way that I learned you had ventured in to Ender Prison, alone. You left Andreas and the paladins to seek the gates while you went in search of your father. Battle was raging in the gorge by then and I could not get to you, so I went seeking another way in.

"How did you know to come for me? Eindal was dead before you ever spoke to him. I knew our bond was strong, but I had done all I could to remain a secret to you. God gave me no knowledge that you would come."

"Perhaps He was protecting us both," I said. "We came in search of an artifact—an orb. We came into possession of Eindal's ledger during our investigation of his death. Andreas recognized the ancient arcane language and we knew it was important, but we didn't have the time to transcribe then.

"You were just a diversion, or so we thought."

The angel laughed. It was such a robust, joyful laugh that I could not help but laugh myself. Andreas came and sat down beside me. He wanted in on the joke with an angel.

"Ah, dear Andreas, Andy as she calls you." She spoke aloud for him.

He nodded, but looked back and forth between us for some clarification of our half spoken conversation.

She continued to speak aloud for Andreas's benefit. "A diversion, you said. It was what The One God said of you when he first sent me to you. *'She will be a diversion for you. Keep her safe'* He kept me waiting for you for ages. He is very particular about which angels he matches with humans. He understood your situation and felt I could keep you safe. You are not my first experience with humans, but you have been the most interesting."

"What situation?"

She did not hide her surprise at my question. "Your father of course. I have been with you your entire life. God and the host knew of him and his want of an heir. There were other—spawn. Heaven's host watched over their lives, but it was you who got Malisgalar's attention. You were strong, determined to survive no matter what. It was your strength that he sought. If he could gain your loyalty he would have a powerful ally and heir. He would have done anything to gain that from you; even brainsickness was not out of the question. He tried to sway you and you struggled with him, although you did not know it at the time. Others did not fare so well and fight against you with the hordes now.

"When you killed him; the first time, and Devil brought him back, he convinced Devil that you were worth whatever it took to bring you under control of his dark ways. You had proven yourself to be strong, smart, and relentless, qualities he admired in his heir.

"The One God knew early on that he would seek you, so he gave me charge of you as your guardian. I watched you grow up. I have cradled you when you cried, afraid of the dark. I fought off many demons that you were never aware of. I held them back for you while you slept."

Even though I knew it in my heart; all I heard after guardian was blah, blah, blah.

When her lips stopped speaking I exclaimed, "You are a guardian, an angel! My—guardian angel?"

"Is it really so hard for you to believe? Have you not felt the connection between us?"

I could not deny that, but I was stunned and did not answer.

"Andreas, do you remember the day that you met Saeede? How you were in a hurry to catch the next ship out?"

He nodded, yes.

"What brought you to change your mind so suddenly and go to the village square where Saeede was just beginning to play?"

"I never knew, really, except that I wanted to go there and play, so I did."

"You are welcome," she said.

"Saeede, since that day your struggle has been eased. The two of you fell in love on your own. Although, I hoped you would have given into it much sooner. You spent so much time dwelling on the dark within you that it was sure to consume you. I thought a companion with like interests would help to keep you from sinking deeper."

I heard her but I felt detached; the memory of so many events came rushing back.

"I knew you even back in Mam's woods."

"Yes, I was there."

"The white raven." It was not a question. I knew the white raven was my protector, at least as a child I liked to think so. Now as an adult I knew I had been right.

"Yes."

"I spoke to you then. Do you remember?"

"Yes, you wanted to share your berries. You have always been a kind heart."

I felt suddenly ashamed and she knew it. I had done some wicked things in my time.

"Don't feel ashamed, Sade. You have a thick skin, thickened by your circumstances. I can tell your heart is still kind."

"You didn't count on Belhanna and Master Eindal then, did you? I feel broken since then."

"No."

There was a pause as she struggled to continue.

"I fought with you at the mage academy, but I lost you for a time after that. I heard about Eindal when I looked for you in Behlanna. By then so much was in place around you that I only knew you were seeking the Hell Gates.

"I was searching for the entrance to Hell in Koman when I came upon a battle between angels and devils. I joined the fight and fell when a cudgel cracked against my head from behind. I was nearly trampled, but managed to crawl to the edge of the field of battle. The battle went against the angels and they fled to save themselves for another battle, another day. I could go no further and blackness over took me. That is how I came to be taken at the asylum. The dark ones move so freely there. They are unchecked.

"You are favored by all of the realms that affect you. Well, until today you were favored by Hell, but I think we can safely say that you are an enemy there now. You are favored by the gods and so you have been blessed on your world."

"You endured so much for me; you were Devil's captive for such a long time. It would have been better for you if you had left me alone."

"And miss the opportunity to do away with your father and save your mother?"

"You knew of that?" I was outraged. "If we are so connected why did you not find a way to let me know my mother's plight sooner?"

"I wanted to."

"But?.. ."

She looked me in the eye; "The host would not allow it. The One God would not allow it. I am bound to Him. He is my king. Your place in this battle between Heaven and Hell had to play out; it is still playing out. If you had known earlier and moved to save your mother all of the pieces would not have been in place. Key players would have been absent. Your mother went to your father to beg him to leave you alone. She knew the danger, but had you gone sooner your mother would not have been there. God can influence people and circumstances, but the outcome is in the hands of Men. I do not dispense hope and I can not heal the sick. That is not my purpose. I cannot predict the future and I certainly do not know the mind of God. Your death or that of your mother would cause me great pain, but I cannot foresee it coming. God found ways to keep her alive and influence the circumstances around her, but her mind was made up. You and Andreas were the method that saved her."

We sat face to face searching the eyes of the other. There was sorrow and pride, strength and remorse, love and worry in her; for me. I could not hide what she saw in my eyes at that moment. A tear fell from her cheek and she reached for my hand.

"Still, there are things that are left undone. My capture was not part of the plan, but once I knew that Malisgaler was back and seeking you again, God knew too. God himself kept me alive then until you could return. Devil and Malisgalar knew the strength of our bond. Every day they took more and more of my spirit into that medallion. Every night they released it in the mountains around the asylum. They thought it would call you to me; perhaps it did. Every night I prayed and God renewed me. I fought in that way until you found your way back.

"The relic you seek was a token given from God. The orb allowed me to go to those places where you needed me in an instant. The veil woven by Devil's minions prevented me from feeling you. The orb is still somewhere in the hands of evil. While it is in the hands of evil God will be quiet. He will not want to reveal more secrets of the orb. But if evil should realize what he has... . I am the one who lost it. I very much want to get it back for Him."

"I have not the strength or ability to go against the legions of Hell. God will have to let this one go."

"You do not understand. When I fought to retrieve the orb at the Mage Academy I saw the one that possessed it. God's Iris is in the hands of a Human."

·~·Chapter Thirteen·~·

"What Human?"

"I do not know. A small little man with a pointed face."

"He was watching the battle from the edges. When I tried to engage him he called out and vanished. I was swarmed by those nearby who laid in wait for you.

"I saw that same man at the edges of the battle in Koman."

Andreas and I knew, "Jest!" We said the name as one voice.

"Good; you know him; then finding him will be easy."

"We sent him away to our own people. If he is a messenger for Devil they are in danger." Andreas said.

"Perhaps he is not a man," I said. "We found clawed foot prints at the place he said you were taken."

"He looks human," Andreas said. "He left boot prints on that day we were with him at the battle field."

"Perhaps he is a lesser demon, a spy for Lord Devil. If that is true everything he told us is a lie, or twisted truth to protect himself."

"Perhaps," the angel said, "I did sense evil, but more like that in a man. It is possible Devil is turning him. Did he have the orb."

"He had a chain around his neck, but it was tucked into his tunic," Andreas said. I grabbed him by the collar once and felt the chain. I don't know if he had anything attached and I didn't think of it then."

"Now that you mention it I recall that the chain was a black metal. Bane Metal, perhaps?" I asked.

"That must be it!" She said. "He could be controlled then."

"We must get to Mareese! Can you fly us there?" I asked.

"Once we get our bearing, yes, but I can not enter there in this form. I have many forms," and she changed to a much shorter woman. Still, she was taller than Andreas. Goodness and light remained with her. She was magnificent to see.

She lamented the condition of her gear. "My armor has seen better days, and I will need weapons. Keeping you from the clutches of evil has not been an easy task."

I was silent as I tried to imagine all that she must have gone through to keep me safe.

Andreas said, "We can see to it that you have new things. What are you called, angel?"

"It is an ancient name given to me by God himself. It means quiet protector. Angels have no gender, but I was given the feminine form of the male name; Fion. I am called Fionaghal," she said with pride.

"Fionaghal," I whispered. "Fionaghal."

"Yes," she said turning to me. "It is so good to hear you pronounce it."

"You are well named." I said. "I am glad to know you at last."

***

Fionaghal landed us gently on the prow of Night's Angel docked in the harbor of Mareese. She changed immediately to her human form.

It was dusk, the time of day when light plays tricks on men's eyes. We padded softly across the deck to the ladder, then down to the berths. Andreas was the last to descend. As he slipped below the level of the deck a drowsy sailor turned his head our way. He walked to the ladder and looked down, but we were already in the shadows of the gangway and moving softly to the captain's door. He did not follow and we heard him walk back to his post, mumbling.

I rapped softly at the captain's door.

"In," he called.

We did as commanded.

"By the gods! You've made it and with time to spare." His eyes went to Fionaghal. "And who is this beauty?" He moved forward and took her hand. "Please forgive me, Dear, but I have never seen such beauty. Welcome to the Night's Angel."

Andreas made introductions, "Fionaghal, Captain Nights— Captain, Fionaghal."

"The name of your ship is Night's Angel?" Fionaghal asked.

Night's nodded.

"What a wonderful name." Her voice was gleeful.

Nights, smiled and kissed her hand. "Your name is even more wonderful."

"Oh brother," I said beneath my breath. "We have come on an urgent matter, Lio. Where is Jest. Did he come with you?"

"He sailed with us here, but he has no desire to work for me. He walked about the city on the first day. I alerted Diony to him as you asked. I washed my hands of him then."

"Is he still in the city?"

"As far as I know. Why? What's wrong?"

"We have reason to believe that he moves against us."

"In what way?"

"There is no time for the full story right now. We must find him before he can wreak more havoc on Mareese," Andreas said.

"How can I help?"

"If you see him do not let him know that we have returned. Do not even tell your men. Should you see him alert the guards and have him detained. We will alert the Governor to the danger."

"There is a watch posted on deck. Can you call him down so that we can slip out unseen?"

"Yes, I can tell him I heard something and then lead him away from you. The crew quarters are empty. The men have gone into town for the night. Wait there, when he comes in here leave quickly."

We stopped and pulled scarves from the carpetbag and wrapped them like turbans around our heads and kept our faces concealed within the front drape. We left the carpetbag with Nights. We would not need anything else from it where we were going.

Night's plan worked and we were soon moving through the foot traffic on the main causeway. We wound our way through town to the gates of the Governor's Manor House.

Fionaghal's accent was foreign enough to fit our cover story. "Please announce to your governor that Andros Sa'de and company have arrived as invited and request an immediate audience with the governor and her advisors."

The guard looked us over. No sign of recognition changed his face at the name given or on sight of us. He sent a squire to announce us. Our wait seemed long, but then the page came at a run. "She says let them come."

The gate was open and we were on safe ground.

Diony and her man, Brynal came across the yard to meet us.

"I'm sorry I made you wait so long. The name Andros Sa'de meant nothing to me. I wondered who would have the audacity to come to the governor's house and feign an invitation. Of course I thought of you right away and then the name made sense. I had already sent the page away and we had to chase him down. Why have you come incognito?"

"We will explain, but not here," Andreas said. Let us walk to somewhere private."

"My office is about as private as it gets." Diony said and motioned us to follow.

Once we were situated we made proper introductions. Then Andreas began our story. I only filled in with small details he forgot to mention, but were important. We withheld the fact that Fionaghal was an angel. They believed us. We knew they did, because they were furious with us for going into Hell without alerting them to it.

Fionaghal remained quiet until the end of the telling and the questions that followed.

"How do you know the horde is on the move again? What about the gates?"

"Devil found a way to pervert the old magic the humans used to keep him imprisoned centuries ago," Andreas said.

Diony was frantic Her short time as Governor of Mareese had been spent dealing with crisis after crisis. "The gates that once held Hell's people back have been undone, again?"

Fionaghal broke her silence. "Had you not noticed that the gates were laced with powers that could drain a human of their soul? There is also a veil between Earth and Hell. It was intact until Sade and Andreas passed through to escape. It was not meant to hold back good souls, but their passing pierced it still. The veil between Hell and Earth has been compromised. It could not be helped. It was the only means of escape left. When the Hellions find it they will swarm out from there."

"What veil? There is another way between the worlds?" Diony plopped down into the chair behind her desk.

"It was only by accident that we found it." Andreas said.

"What is it that you are not telling me? Surely there is not an entrance to hell through Breen? Where did you escape from?"

Reluctantly we told Diony, her security chief, Ray Mac Ven, and her Lord Protector, Brynal that part of the story. We continued to leave out that Fionaghal was an angel, but in the end they believed us. We knew they did, because they became more angry.

"The veil is only compromised in the spot where they came through," Fionaghal said. "There is still a chance that Earth is safe."

Diony leveled her most displeased look at Fionaghal. The angel shied and shrugged her shoulders like a chastised child. Diony is a force of her own.

"I must act on the chance that it is *not* safe. Tell me where exactly is this breech."

"In the mountains near Pyritia," I said.

"At least we are safe for now. I will alert the government there and offer what aid we can."

"What about this man Jest?" Ray Mac Ven asked.

"We believe he has an orb. God's Iris, Eindal called it. Eindal spoke to Jest about it and recorded it in a journal that we possess. After speaking to Jest it is not clear who initiated the conversation. It is even possible that Jest killed Eindal himself for the purpose of obtaining that ledger. The ledger reads a lot like a journal. It may have been the real reason he was killed. In addition to the scroll keys, the Hell gates, and the orb there is information about many places, people and things of great power. Jest acted as a guide for Eindal when Eindal was in Koman. We believe that he is some sort of a messenger for the forces of evil, or maybe just a pawn" Andreas explained.

"So you sent him here?!"

"We did not suspect him then. He helped us to find Fionaghal. It turns out that was just another plot to lure Sade in so her father could have another go at turning her." Andreas replied.

"I doubt Jest is still here," I said. "More likely he has returned to his masters."

"I have not seen him here," Ray said. "I left orders with the guard to report any trouble he causes. There has been none so far. Perhaps you are right and he has left the city already."

I was suddenly alarmed; "Or gone to Breen," I said.

"No," Fionaghal said. "If he has the orb he will look for the shortest route back to the Hells. Enders Prison is the closest way from here. We must go quickly."

Diony sighed, "Do you have anything you would like me to say at the treaty council on your behalf?"

"We still have time," Andreas told her, "but if we are not here, tell them we are off to save the world for all Men."

"So dramatic." She said scornfully.

"Minstrel's Privilege."

"Is that a thing?" She asked.

"Of course. You've never heard of it?"

Of course she hadn't since he had just made it up.

"Go save the world, Minstrels. I'll alert the heads of countries for you; like I always do."

We bowed to her and left before we made her more distraught and angry than we already had.

We had one last thing to do and that was to see that Fionaghal was properly armed and armored. We could purchase weapons that would suit her, but armor was going to be difficult without revealing her true nature. We had learned a few things working for the smithies in Breen. If we could get access to a forge and anvil we felt that we could fashion something that would serve her well.

Ray Mac Ven had been a blacksmith before serving as Diony's sheriff. He had been willing to help us without Diony's consent in the past. We waited for him outside of Diony's office and asked for access to the governor's armory and smithy. He was cautious at first, but he could see that Fionaghal was in need of armor and weapons. He led us to the armory where Fionaghal picked two great swords and two sets of armor. Ray was curious and wanted to assist us, but to our good fortune he was called away.

I shut and barred the smithy doors and we went to work. A few hours later we had a suit of armor that fit Fionaghal's natural size. She worked her transformation and appeared as her human form again; armor and all. We banked the coals in the forge and slipped away from the smithy un-noticed.

***

The hidden ways through the city of Mareese are many, but known only to a few. Andreas and I are among those few. We came off the rogues highway only long enough to have Fionaghal make a purchase of instruments for us. A flute for me, a harp for Andreas, and rhythm sticks for her.

From there we made our way to a net makers shop. The building was near the main causeway that leads up into the city from the wharf. We huddled in the shadows below the nets that hang between his shop and home on the quay side of the wharf. We were well hidden but kept our voices low.

I was tired and frustrated; "I grow weary of this chase," I said. "Back and forth, forth and back. What clues do we actually have about the orb?"

Andreas listed them, "Eindal's Ledger and the description of the orb including the possibility of an angel, which we have successfully proven exists. There are Lily's notes, but I have yet to know how they figure in all of this. There is the rock shard with the words 'Come, Sade', at the spot where Jest said Fionaghal was taken.

That seems so obvious now that he was urging us on. I bet Jest was frustrated when we didn't find it our first time through. It must be the reason he tried so hard to accompany us. He was very surprised when we showed up on his doorstep. He must have rejoiced when we asked him to lead us to the battleground.

"We have your testament, Fionaghal, that you sensed the man with the orb in the area at the time of your abduction, though we now believe he is a man being turned to a demon. That little bastard played us well, he sent us right back into their hive to rescue you. He knew that we would.

"Your father still being alive—or again, and pleading for you to join him was a surprise. We fooled them though, didn't we? They had no revenge, and we took their bait—Fionaghal, but not in the way they expected.

"Fionaghal fought and fell unconscious at the Mage Academy. When they left you I imagine Devil was not too happy. That is why they swarmed and chased you each time after that; even as you retreated. They had orders to capture you. That would allow them revenge upon Saeede. I no longer think they know about the orb. I believe Jest is alone in that. He planted that rock shard which allowed him to live up to his bargain to aid Devil and Saeede's father. The orb is a happy circumstance for him. A power play of some sort, or a way out perhaps."

I agreed. "That theory does have merit. Fionaghal, what would God do if Jest used the orb? Would He know it was used?"

"Yes. His powers are instilled in the orb, to be used by His messengers. His messengers can to speak to Him telepathically through it. If Jest used it in that way he might feel God's presence on the other end. God would have to have a very good reason to want to enter conversation with a man of evil. I believe He would remain silent."

"We know that Jest has vanished from you, so he knows that power at least. Our information tells us of only these abilities: to speak and hear God, and to travel ethereally through the cosmos; whatever the cosmos are. Do you know anymore than that?"

"No, what you have said is accurate. The cosmos are those worlds created by God and watched over by the lesser gods and the angels. There are many worlds in the cosmos, another name is universe. There are many Earths in the universe. In the most ancient language earth means life. The One God is the master of them all.

"If there is more, only God knows it. I know God would reveal them to me if it meant our safety. On the other hand he would not—if it meant our safety."

"Why would Devil bother with the intrigues of man and lesser devils?" Andreas asked.

"To weaken God; then overpower Him. I doubt that is even possible, but Devil is not right in his head. Devil was one of God's host, but he was ill-minded, weak spirited, and fell to greed. He wanted what only God can fully comprehend. They fought and Devil was cast down to this world –into the mantel of the planet. He was trapped there. His ravings manifested in the forms of devils and demons, and they did not know God. There is also an inherent evil in Man that some cannot control. When they commit an evil act a shard of their soul spills out of them and that shard of evil becomes a demon. Most often it will attach to that person and tease them into more evil and torment their goodness until they die or are killed for their evil ways. When the host dies the demons seek the evil of others whether they be man, beast, or companion demons. Sometimes they will choose to go alone into the world and seek a place or thing or person through which they can manipulate minds and events. They are drawn to evil. Many have already found their way to Lord Devil. He gathers them as a force and then sends them out into your world in search of others of their kind. Your world has become over-run with Men possessed by demons. These men and demons bring foul, unspeakable evil to your world.

"Good men fought them back. Great leaders lost their lives to seal them back into the depths. They built and magiked the gates and created the veil as a secondary fence. As you know now, magic can be perverted and veils can be torn.

"Still, the gates were successful for a time, but demons had already taken their toll on the souls and minds of men. Some demons escaped capture and walked the lands as men. Your father was one, for a time. He did love you in his own way. He had revealed himself to your mother. He offered her to be his concubine. She was repulsed and denied him. He let her live. He must have loved her then, others that refused him did not survive. At your birth he let down his guard. When he did; three angel's found him and before he could escape they cast him back into the mantel. He did not leave you willingly.

"You continue that fight against Devil. He needs many powerful demons and devils if he is ever to bring down the host of heaven. *That* is why he teases at the minds and souls of Man.

"Devil has never ventured out. He knows God watches him, and will kill him if he does. Still, if The Iris falls into his hands his great intelligence would not take long to work the power it holds. He could escape us time and again."

"Tell us more about why you had the Iris."

"I was to use it to protect you. God feared a cataclysm if Andreas used his power over the elements against the prime evil of Devil himself. I was to take you away if that happened."

"That seems to have worked out as planned," I said.

Fionaghal smiled.

"Is that all?" Andreas asked.

"Both of you are favored by the gods, and the One God is fond of both of you. The Iris was to keep us safe, a shelter if Devil was upon us. A safe place until God could remove us from harm. He would not have been long. He wants nothing to happen to either of you, but it is you Saeede that draws *His* attention."

"I cannot imagine why." I asked.

"There will be a time that He will need warriors among men. To lead them. He has the heavenly host, but Man is not so trusting. You, were not so trusting, but always you kept to the good just for the sake of it. God will need good men to fight along side the angels if evil is ever to be undone, for good."

"You will know what to say to men to bring them to God's army when He has need of it." Andreas added.

"What is the heavenly host?" I asked Fionaghal.

"The army of God, the angels, and lesser gods. God is our General. As angel's we carry out his orders. There are angel's, like me, who are assigned to protect those good children who are being pursued by evil, like you, Saeede. There are other angels whose duty it is to bring death or judgment, among other things. The army of God is invisible to man unless we choose to appear; or we are weakened by Devil's necromancer."

Most of my life I denied God. I believed, a good god would not allow the evil things that I had seen and experienced. I said nothing about that to Fionaghal, but she knew.

"Yet always you always held on to what was good. You champion good and the people you help are lifted up and come to God through you. You are not so blind that you do not know that."

It was true. I knew that something of what I did, made light in the dark world in which we live. There was a glimmer that I kept suppressed, that I hoped my actions would be for the gods or if possible to the One God, if he existed. I just never felt that I was

162

worthy. That the daughter of a witch and a demon could be loved by God never seemed likely.

"The demons have used your doubt against you. It is what they do," Fionaghal said. "They use your sins, and the sins of those around you; the sins others have committed against you, and they spin them into doubt and self loathing. You think that God could not love you or accept you. Do you not know that he calls Men his children? What better love is there than that of a father?"

"I wouldn't know." I snapped.

Fionaghal sighed, she was sorry for her choice of words but she did not apologize. "He will give everything to save his children," she said.

"God has no place for your father, but he does not appall your mother because she does good in the world. He cries out for her. He has sorrow that she does not know Him as He truly is. Other gods know her and praise her, but she has not let the One God in. Perhaps she will after this."

"She keeps much to herself, to protect me. I wager that she knows Him."

Fionaghal nodded, hoping that could be true.

"There will come a time; I think it will be soon; that we will part ways. I will miss you, but I have learned much from you. You need not fear, Saeede. God is with you."

I could not believe the sense of loss at hearing those words from her. I looked at her and tears came up in my eyes. She had fought for me and kept me safe all of my life. Now just when I was ready and able to accept such things she announced that our time would be short.

She moved close and put her arms around me. The embrace was like the passing of a lifetime. All that was good in my life flooded my spirit. It was a shock of love and enlightenment. It was

163

the comfort I had felt when I slept in dark woods, the strength when I thought I could not go on, and the love for strangers when I despised humanity.

"Remember," she said, "and you will never be without me. I will remember too, and you will always be with me when *I* am tired and afraid."

Andreas broke the moment in his usual cavalier way. "I hate to break up this love-fest, but shouldn't we be theorizing, strategizing and mobilizing?"

"Of course," Fionaghal said.

"Alright then, let's start with Jest and work our way back to when we decided to do this thing. What do we know about him?"

I thought about the pointy nosed little man. "We don't trust him. His whole demeanor is fawning, but something about the way he looks at us seems crafty. Eindal gained information about the orb from Jest."

"Did Jest tell Eindal about the orb or did Eindal ask Jest about it?" Andreas wondered. "Eindal mentions Jest in the ledger, but who actually gained from their encounters; Eindal, or Jest? Did Eindal trust him? I think it is more likely that once Jest heard about the orb from Eindal's inquiries he went in search of it himself, following Devil's troops and not, as we assumed, hunkering down in Koman begging for a way off."

"So his luck pans out and he is there when you try to divert Devil's spies away from us. During a battle Jest scrambles to pick up the fallen orb. Even he can't believe his luck when he gets his hands on it. Depending on how much Eindal trusted him is how much Jest knows about the properties of the orb. I think Eindal was a cautious man and knowing that he was also searching for Hell Gates and Gate scrolls I doubt he would have said much."

"If we assume, as we are, that Jest has absconded with the orb then perhaps that was his only plan all along. He was a poor soul trapped on Koman and was looking for any way he could to get off. I don't believe he is trust worthy, but I think he was just biding his time waiting for an opportunity. Eindal was looking for his opportunities at the asylum. Eindal was a source of information to Jest, so he looked for his opportunity at the asylum too. When the spies went out Jest went with them. We all just played into his life, and he acted," I said.

"As simple as that?" Andreas was doubtful.

"I think so."

"If he does possess the orb do you think he knows what he has?"

Fionaghal spoke up, "As I struggled to follow my brethren from the field of battle I felt someone close to me—following. I recognized the spirit. For a brief moment I hoped it was you, Saeede. I reached out to find your spirit but reeled at what I found instead. The person who followed me was evil. They were highly intelligent, but their mind was twisted with deceptions. I broke contact almost immediately for fear the person would detect me, but I did recognize the spirit. It was the one at the Mage's Academy; the one with the orb. The contact as brief as it was caused me pain and my struggle deepened. I could not keep up and I succumbed to my weakened state. I think that person alerted the devils to me. I believe you are right; that this Jest is the person with the orb."

"It fits what we know of the day that you were taken." I said.

Andreas agreed, "He was very knowledgeable of the events. It would be a simple thing for him to fabricate the story as if he was an observer rather than a participant."

"But are we assuming too much?" I wondered.

"I am sure that the one who followed me was the one who had vanished from me at the Mage Academy," she repeated emphatically.

"Alright," Andreas began again, "we are convinced that Jest has it. Captain Nights confirms that Jest traveled with him to Mareese. He alerted Diony and Ray MacVen of that, but Ray believes he has left the city. If you were an opportunistic prig and you had in your possession, an orb belonging to an angel where would you go? Who would you know to talk to, to find out what the thing does?"

We contemplated all that we had discussed. I broke the silence, "If we put events in order then Jest must have been in possession of the orb even before he had conversations with Eindal about it. I even begin to like him for Eindal's murder."

"Why would he kill Eindal if he wanted us to know about Fionaghal and the orb?"

"To buy time. He knew Eindal would write the information in the ledger, perhaps he even witnessed him do it." Andreas stopped suddenly. He was recalling some detail. "My God, do you remember that night that I snuck into Eindal's room? I told you that I had scared someone away. I thought it was odd that A procurer of rare items would hide his secret ledger under the mattress and yet there it was. What if... ."

"I remember," I said. "What if the murderer had the ledger and wanted us to find it? If that was Jest that you scared away that night, and he had the orb, you did not see him run down the alley, because he vanished."

"It would explain the void in the blood we saw that day, but could never fully explain. Eindal wasn't killed for the scrolls, he was killed for the ledger, *and* the scrolls."

"Oh this is so much deeper, so much richer than when we thought only the scrolls were in play."

We took a moment to let that sink in, then I tried to get us back on track.

"Trying to put myself in his shoes," I said, "I have this orb. I assume it is the orb Eindal searched for and I know that it belongs to the angel in Devil's custody. I hide it away and try to find out more. If I had the ledger only a few hours after Eindal's death there would not have been enough time to decipher it, even if I was versed in arcane languages. But, we know that he has used the vanishing ability because Fionaghal has seen him do it. He must have seen you use it during those times you tried to protect us before we went to visit the duke.

"He also was present when Fionaghal was captured. So I imagine he would be worried that she would reveal the orbs existence under Devil's tortures. It is part of the reason he spends so much time lurking about in the mountains around the asylum. As time passes, and there is not a full out search being conducted he begins to feel safe.

"Since the orb belonged to an angel any other powers it held would be for good and not evil. He could begin to think only of things that an angel might need an orb of magic to do. I don't think it would take me long to come up with a list of the most probable.

"Then I meet two minstrel's with a ship. I don't need the ship, I can go anywhere."

"Only places known to him, or that God sends him," Fionaghal said.

"Okay, he's been around with the spies trying to stop us from gaining the scrolls. Let's say he has been to Mareese. We know he is evil, a liar, and perhaps a demon." I stopped to think before continuing.

"What if he is already close to Devil? He is still a duplicitous cur. Is he keeping the orb to himself? What if he is still playing us?"

"How?" Andreas wanted to know.

"Wouldn't I be a sweet token to lay before Devil if someone was trying to win his favor?"

Now Andreas took up the thread. "If that is the case I would want to stay close somehow. We wouldn't take him up on his guide offer, but we do offer him passage to anywhere he wants to go. If we are right about all of this then he would have to know who we are. He knew us when we first saw him. He's good."

"Mareese is a good place to keep an eye on us. Have you ever seen him there before?" I asked.

"I don't think so," Andreas said. "If he ever was he still couldn't have known we were going to Koman; could he?" He looked to Fionaghal for an answer.

"I do not know. His spirit is too hard to read. He is so full of deceptions; I believe anything could be possible with this one, especially if Devil supports him." Fionaghal's statement sent a shiver down our spines. The implications were enormous.

We searched each others faces, hoping to find some clarity in all that we considered. It was so scattered with pieces coming into focus from years ago, but it was there. It was starting to make sense.

Andreas gathered our focus back. "Back to what his plan is for the orb."

"If I am an opportunistic prig and have an orb belonging to an angel—I would go to the Academy of Sages," I said.

"Good thinking," he said. "That is certainly worth a try."

***

We waited in a parlor set aside for the leisure of the Academy's fellows. Several members of the teaching body filed in and out. A few stayed to read or meditate, while another made polite conversation.

Finally Master Eble, The High Elder of the school, came in. Eble had recently celebrated his seventy second birthday. Decades of physical and mental training kept him younger than his years. Still sharp of mind and fit in body he strode gracefully in and greeted us warmly. Eble had tutored me in the past to control my cursed chill. We attempted to control the violent growl, but that was not as succesful. One look at me showed his concern for our presence in his school that night. He took us to a table in a secluded corner of the parlor.

"I had heard you moved to your holdings in Breen. What brings you back to Mareese so soon? The treaty conference isn't for another two months yet. Why the disguises?"

"I haven't told my mother that we are back, and I don't expect that we will be able to stay. We are on a dire mission. It's also possible that there are spies who seek to have me killed."

He sighed, his mouth dropped, and in that instant I saw the aged man revealed behind his outer countenance. It was a flash and then gone. "Will it always be that way with you two?"

I let my exhaustion show in my expression. "It is not a position that we seek, but somehow it always seems to find us." I said.

His eyes softened and there was sympathy in them. "I will help you if I can."

After a few questions we learned that there had been a man asking about an ancient religious relic said to be brought to Earth by an angel from heaven. Eble had not been the one to speak to him. "I will take you to him. He resides here at the academy. He is a religious scholar and seemed the best choice to answer the man's questions. Follow me," Eble stood without another word and we followed him out of the parlor and down the hall.

The man we were going to see was a monk named Eli. He had come to the academy after hordes of demons had swarmed the city three years ago. He was educated in the works of many religions and offered his help to banish strays from the city. He stayed on to teach at the academy in exchange for room and board.

Eble knocked on the apartment door. A slight little man opened it wide. On seeing Eble his smile grew and he beckoned us in. When he saw Fionaghal he stepped back as if he recognized her. A gasp escaped his lips and he bowed to her.

Fionaghal was as much surprised as the rest of us. "Do I know you, Sirrah?"

"I hoped you did. I see you, but do not know you. How is it that you are here? Sweet angel, what has happened that you come as a mortal to my door?"

Eble whispered. "What?" He looked Fionaghal over with renewed interest.

Eli answered, "I have seen angels all of my life."

"My true form is apparent to you?"

"Like an apparition. It surrounds you and you walk within your true form."

Angel and monk gazed long upon each other while we all watched on in our own amazement. Fionaghal was the first to speak again. "I trust you Eli. You have a good soul. We must talk to you about the man who came asking about orbs and angels."

"Oh no, have I done something wrong?"

"If you have it would not be your fault."

"I was so happy to share what I know of angels. So few people believe me, but he was anxious to hear all that I knew."

"What was his interest in the orb he mentioned?"

"I could not help him with it. I had never come across such a thing in all of my reading."

"Did he show it to you?"

"No. He was a student of religion on a quest to find the thing and return it to his masters. Does such a thing truly exist?"

Fionaghal was asking all the right questions. She answered his with another, "Did he specify what an angel's orb might do if one existed?"

"He asked; he didn't know specifics. I speculated that it might just be a symbol of station. Like a prince among angels."

"What did he say to that?"

"He seemed disappointed."

"Did you offer any more speculations?"

"I thought it might be a boon from God for a favored minion."

"What was his reaction to that?"

"He seemed pleased."

"Did you or he venture any guesses as to what type of boon that might be?"

"Who is this man that you are so concerned about what he thinks about a rhetorical orb?"

"Please answer, Eli and I will tell you what I can after."

"We tossed around some ideas; healing, communication, empathy with Earth bound mortals, punishment to mortals, divining."

"Did he seem especially interested in any of those possibilities?"

"No, no. He took them all into consideration."

"Please angel, tell me what this all means."

"Only because you are a godly man. Events have taken place that have caused a tear in the veil between worlds. Heaven is safe, for now, but denizens of Hell will soon find their way upon the Earth once again, if they have not already. You will know of that soon enough as men move to combat that. These things happened because an angel became separated from her charge and the charge was surrounded by evil forces that played against her and the angel The evil pulled at the poor mortal soul and nearly had her twice."

Eble understood her meaning and grasped my hand. When I looked at him I saw a tear come up in his eye.

Fionaghal was saying, "Where the mortal escaped, the angel did not and she was captured by their lord, Devil. The mortals stumbled upon the angel and pulled her from the grip of the Devil himself. Before the angel was lost to the Devil she lost an item, an orb. We believe the man you spoke with has found it and seeks to use it for his own evil game, or gain, or both."

"And you were that angel?"

She looked the man in the eye, weighing whether she should answer.

Eli looked to Andreas and I, "and one of you?.. ."

Andreas entered into the questioning of the monk. "Did he say where he was going?"

"No, but I did suggest that if he knew the angel's purpose here that he might then have some clue to the orb's purpose." Eli hung his head as the magnitude of what he had done sank in. "I was so excited that there might be physical proof of an angel being present here on Earth, I offered to go with him on his search. He was so kind a man, and said he would contact me if he found it and we could work together to reveal the powers of it." Eli shuddered, "I did not stop to think he might be using me for an evil purpose."

"No one blames you, Eli, but now that you know... ." Andreas's words were interrupted.

"I won't speak of it again, ever."

"Good. Speak not of me as well." Fionaghal said.

Eli nodded to affirm.

Fionaghal looked to Eble. He understood and nodded as well.

"Are we done here?" Fionaghal asked Andreas and I.

Nodding seemed to be the appropriate answer. The angel had commanded the scene and we had a good idea that Jest would return to Hell to forge a deal with Devil; with information about us in exchange for the orb. If he was as cunning as we expected he might even leverage a position. With Malisgalar and the necromancer gone Devil could use another henchman.

"We will show ourselves out, Ebel," I said. "I am sure that you and Eli have a lot to talk about. Expect Diony to seek you out about protecting the veil. Perhaps Eli's knowledge can be of help there."

He hugged me, then we shook hands with our hosts and left.

·~·Chapter Fourteen·~·

We traveled through the secrets ways above and below Mareese until we came out near the Jagged Spires. We moved into the natural bowl that the stone spires surrounded to conceal ourselves from travelers on the road. We had little hope of finding signs of Jest's passing but we had to try. The traffic was light at that late hour and during a gap between travelers I went down to the road and attempted to pick up Jest's trail while Andreas and Fionaghal remained hidden.

I was as unsuccessful as we had predicted, but at least we had not passed on an opportunity.

We passed through the southern arm of the spires, and into the mountains along the Larol Pass. It was there that we made a fortunate discovery; three soft booted human footprints with the telltale impression of clawed toes moving in the same direction We were tired and had hoped to make a cold camp there, but this trail was already old and the ground was difficult for tracking. We pushed on.

We lost and picked up the trail several times along the rocky Larol Pass. At the road the prints were obliterated by days of traffic but they had exited the pass on a heading that would take them across the road and into the desert on the other side. Ender Prison laid in that direction.

We crossed the road and moved into a region called The Vale, along the eastern edge of the Desert. Jest's trail was lost, erased by winds across the sands. It was approaching evening. We made camp in one of many caves within The Vale. In the morning we suffered the heat of day and crossed the desert.

We found the old camp above Ender Prison. It is situated in a long, narrow furrow at the southern edge of the desert. A wide slope leads down from the desert into the northern end of the camp. The eastern access is rocky, the west is closed off by foothills and stepped down in elevation to the wall at the south end of the furrow. Those foothills offered a good defensible position if we needed one. The south wall of the furrow is not as steep, but no less jagged. The prison was situated in a deep gorge at the south end of the furrow.

We made our way up through the rocks of the foothills to a concealed edge that looked out over the gorge where Ender Prison stood. It was the best place to survey the prison. We saw signs of a disturbance in the rocks and soil there. An indication that Jest had lain much as we did and watched the activity at the prison.

The prison gorge was deep and closed in around the building. The walls of it became part of the building. It appeared as if the prison grew right up out of the ground in the southwest corner of the ravine. A high curved wall formed the boundary of a small yard. Glass and stone were set into the top of the wall all around. A heavy wood beamed door bound with darkening iron was the only obvious entrance, but we knew another way. A natural spring produced an oasis on the edge of the ravine. It spilled over the eastern wall of the ravine and sloughed across the small yard inside the prison gates, barely flowing. Once barred openings along the buildings foundation were now filled with stone blocks and mortar. It was through those blocked windows that we had left the prison on our return to Mareese.

A small contingent of men combined of volunteers from Mareese, Ge, and Jour walked the upper walls at regular intervals. Two stood stationary at either side of the entrance gate and two stood on the roof above the door. We watched, afraid to move from fear of being discovered.

When night fell we did move along the ridge to the western edge of the prison ravine. We climbed down to a broad plateau and moved across it to the southeast. This brought us to the south side of the prison and the oasis at the southern rim of the ravine. We moved carefully through the flow of water that spilled over the rim into the courtyard below. We were at a corner between building and mountain where we could climb down the wall or cliff or both at once if we pleased. A quick check of the guard positions told us that the time to move was then. We climbed down quickly into the flow of water backed up against the wall. The foundation was under water here as the water moved slowly to an unseen outlet. The sealed windows at ground level prevented the flow from entering the building. The window nearest to us had been sealed by Andreas before we left the prison only a day before.

Fionaghal and I pressed our backs against the wall of the prison and watched over our shoulders for guards while Andreas carefully removed and stacked the stone blocks beside the window. The sound of falling water was loud and I was sure it would bring the attention of the guards. We moved quickly. I slid in first and then helped Fionaghal in. Andreas was last. There was no call from the guards above, but the room where we stood was flooded once again.

The flow of water had to be stopped. Andreas put the stone blocks back into place and using the energy in the blocks of stones he created a strong seal. The flow of water stopped.

We led the angel through the prison. We avoided contact simply by acting as if we belonged there. No one stopped us or called out and we were soon descending the narrow flight of stairs that led to the gate.

We played the key on our instruments and moved in. We locked the gate with the proper notes and I led the way to the ruins of Malisgalar's lair. From there we would be able to see the mountain rising at the center of three realms. At the mountain we would climb down to the Devil's realm in search of Jest and the orb.

I started out across the foggy ground.

The fog followed. We could not afford to have Andreas spend his energy to combat what was just an unsettling annoyance. We endured the clinging fog and moved on.

We came to where the traitor, Sardon and my father's minion froze the fugitive, Polk. Polk who was known to the denizens of Hell as Polqutis, still stood, frozen and dead. If a mere minion of Hell could do this what could Lord Devil do? We had beaten him back once and escaped with Fionaghal's help, but what would he, could he do, if he got a hold of us again?

I had been hidden in the fog when the minion grabbed the throat of Polqutis. The cold of his touch spread and froze the man to death. He pulled his hand from the futile frozen grip of his victim and turned from Polqutis. When he did he walked away with his lover, Sardon.

I had followed them then, so I knew the way.

On that day I had a gift from the dwarves to protect me from un-death. We did not have them now. They had been taken by the necromancers henchmen when they put Andreas into the ossuary niche.

I took a deep breath of the frosty air and exhaled slowly. I was reassured by the warm cloud of breath I expelled. "If that stops we are in trouble," I said.

I stepped forward in the direction that the minion and Sardon had gone on that day. Andreas and Fionaghal followed. Distant sounds came to our ears, but we could not sort them. I made my turns with the help of my memory but the further we moved into the fog the more our senses became muddled. I hesitated each time, unsure of myself but my memory was true, and I chose rightly.

I smiled and thanked the god's and God again for circumstance. My spirit trembled. Something in that thanksgiving sat badly with me. I was not a godly person and they knew it. It was not good to offend the gods while standing in Hell.

I pushed those thoughts aside and looked across the great black river from the same spot I had stood upon two years ago. I was weak and wracked with the chill then. I was weakened again, from fatigue, and emotionally vulnerable, but the chill was mostly under control.

The great river before us was broad and smooth. Black fog rose from the black water. Across the river a tangle of broken towers rose from the fog. No light came from any windows, just as it had been on that day before the towers fell. I walked the shore in search of the boat I knew should be there. It was and I was glad. I would not be forced to swim the cold and acrid waters of that black river again.

Fionaghal offered another way across. She took us up into her powerful arms and we glided just above the water. She set us down gently on the other side.

"Better to leave the boat where it is and not have the owners wonder why the boat is not where they left it," Fionaghal said.

We gathered behind bushes on a low bank of the river. We could only hear the rush of the river. We could see nothing but black— black ground, black sky, black river, and black trees.

"I feel as if there are eyes upon us." Andreas whispered.

"I had that same feeling when I was here before." I replied. "Let's move away from the river. It unnerves me."

We had torches that we could use, but they would be a beacon of our presence. We were wary of horde remnants on the move.

We made our way in the dark to the landmark of Malisgalar's fallen towers. The mountain rose up behind it. The dark shape was barely perceptible against the dark sky. In that mountain Andreas and the paladins had found there way to the unlocked Hell Gates while I made my way to Malisgalar, my father. Had we known then the true nature of the mountain much of our perception of Hell would have been changed.

Andreas lead us from the fallen towers and we found the gate quickly. We played the key softly to open and then relock the gate before we made our way down into the last tier of Hell. We made our way cautiously, on foot, to the rim of the flat top mountains overlooking the plaza in the necropolis of Lord Devil.

It hummed with the activity of an army preparing to deploy. We saw no sign of Devil. As powerful a creature as he was, he lived in great fear of his creator. We had sparked his fear. He thought we came to deliver the wrath of God upon him. That was absurd. We had acted as mortals, desperate to survive. I prayed our desperation and the aid of one angel would be enough to get us through again.

From our vantage point we could not see into the arena. There was only one way that we could cross and avoid a battle in the courtyard. Fionaghal would have to fly us into the bowl of the arena. That left us vulnerable to the arrows of archers if we were detected.

While Andreas and I assessed our situation Fionaghal sat in meditation. She searched for the aura of the man she had sensed nearby during her abduction. When that failed she attempted to feel the orb. When that failed she prayed to God. We crouched beside her watching for any signs that we had been sighted. After a long time she opened her eyes and sadly shook her head, no.

We reclined among the rocks with our weapons resting on our bellies. Whispering together we formulated a plan. Lord Devil resided somewhere in the oddly constructed building that surrounded the arena. We knew that Jest was days ahead of us. We believed he was attempting to play into Devil's favor. It was possible that he had reached Lord Devil already. They could be anywhere by then, but the arena was a good place to start looking.

We wanted the orb, no matter who possessed it. To get beyond the plaza and into the arena we would have to fly and risk detection. Fionaghal was our best chance to make it. She could change her form to appear as anything she wished. We settled on something resembling the necromancer. A shadowy form in flowing robes. We hoped the troops below would see us as just another evil thing if we were sighted. We relied on Andreas and his ability to bend light to conceal us in her arms. We would fly directly into the arena and land on the main concourse. Once inside we would battle what ever we encountered until we found the orb, or died trying.

When we flew above Devil's army many dark soldiers pointed to the sky. A cheer went up. Our disguise worked. Fionaghal circled once around for effect and then swept down onto the main concourse of the arena.

The arena was empty of life, but the body of the necromancer still lay in a heap where it had fallen, and puddles of water still indicated where my father had met his end.

We made our way down to the stage and began our search there. There was no sign of Devil, Jest, or the orb. We began an orderly sweep from the bottom, up. We searched the stage, the arena, and the seating, before entering into the doors and archways in the walls at the floor of the arena.

We went floor by floor. This was Devil's palace. The interior rooms were well appointed. The arena was his playground. We encountered household staff, consorts, and henchmen. We did not discriminate when it came to dispatching them. Fionaghal was a mighty warrior and her wrath was felt by all that we encountered.

***

While we were moving across the desert on our way to Ender Prison, Diony was busy sending messages and men to the people of Pyritium. Eli and Eble were among them. Diony's small army was complemented with volunteers from Ge. Their duke, Tourabain, was in command. Diony ordered Captain Nights who had one of the fastest ships in the harbor to sail them to the small island of Pyr upon which the city of Pyritium was built. Another ship sailed with supplies and the overflow of men.

Eble and Eli went as representatives into the city. They were not well received. The people of Pyritium had great skill at forging weapons and armor. Many of the island states around them traded for the quality of their work or sent their youngsters to learn the craft from the masters on Pyr. The respect for their weapons was enough to keep most invaders away. The people of Pyr had never had to test their weapons against an army of men. The Hell Gate in their slums was the one that had never been unlocked. Hordes of demons would test them to epic proportion and they did not wish to share the glory of that.

They scoffed at Eble's offers of aid and calls for support, until the demon guerrillas began to wreak havoc upon them. They quickly realized that even their armor and weapons could not stand against the powers and sheer numbers of the Hellish Hordes.

Eli eased tensions between the army of Crystalier and the people of Pyritium. The weapon and armor artisans of Pyritium supplemented the inferior armor and weapons of the Mareesians and many armed, strong, men and women of Pyr joined them on their march to seal the veil.

·~·Chapter Fifteen·~·

We spent hours systematically searching and battling our way up through the chambers of the arena. We entered onto a colonnade that ran part way along the top edge of the arena. From there we could look down into the plaza on one side, or the arena on the other. To our left the colonnade ended. To our right it went one quarter of the way around the arena. A stout door constructed of various metal bands blocked our way at that point. In front of the door an intimidating guard stood to keep us from the door.

The guard held a spiked cudgel in one hand and had a spiked buckler strapped to the other arm. The horned black helmet gleamed in the light coming through the colonnade. A black horn protruded from each side of the helmet just above the ears. These horns were turned down and could do no harm. It was the horn that protruded straight out from the top of the visor that could be lethal. Every horn was tipped with the glassy black metal. He wore the scarlet robes; that were the livery of Devil's household guards, over field plate armor. Over the robes he wore pauldrons of layered plates. The top plates were fashioned with metal spikes that stood straight up. If the guard lowered a shoulder in battle it would be very bad for the recipient of that hit. Around his waist a thick black girdle was fit with several thin poniards. The beast was a walking killing machine.

The eyes glowed behind the visor and the guard watched as we strode toward him. It was the black magic in his eyes that put Andreas behind Fionaghal and I, from there he could watch and attempt to counter any magic that came at us. He was nervous, he would have to be quick and exact about his counter measures. Any miscalculation against dark magic could be deadly, or worse—excruciating. Fionaghal and I had to be aware of our positions in front of Andreas not only to protect him, but to be within his circle of protection.

Fionaghal spoke in a deep, hushed voice and tried to influence the mind of the spectral guard before us. She failed and he swung his weapon once above his head in one swift motion.

I did not wait to see if this was a threat or an attack. I lunged forward and jammed one silver scimitar after the other upward beneath the fauld and between the fassets. His huge body writhed and twisted as he fell toward me. I would have been forced over the low wall of the colonnade had Fionaghal not stopped him and pushed him back. He was not dead, only wounded. I pulled my weapons from his belly. They did not drip with blood, but smoked as if they had been dipped in acid. He fell to his knees before the heavy metal door he guarded. His head rolled back as he fought against the pain. Before he could gather his wits out of the shock he was experiencing and cry out I ran my blades into his neck at intersecting angles and severed his spine. The body imploded beneath me and the armor clanged against the ground.

We gathered close together and knelt below the level of the low wall that supported the columns. We were back, to back, to back; a triangle able to view an advance from any direction The implosion had not been very loud, but we were ready for an advance if one came. The noise in the plaza covered anything they could have heard from there. The arena was empty. No attack came. We turned our attention back to the door.

We huddled at the threshold to Devil's domicile in the highest tier of the irregular blocks structure. It seemed unlikely that he would have only one guard there. He had a devious mind. One guard might make us feel superior to his forces, so that we would barge into a trap beyond that door.

We knew better. Either Devil was elsewhere commanding his troops or we were about to enter into a powerful melee that we could not plan for. Devil had many demons with varied powers at his disposal. We would face whatever he put before us and push on.

Fionaghal stood at her full height just inside the cover of shadow that the roof of the colonnade afforded us. Andreas and I stayed low as we worked the door. If anyone looked our way they would see Fionaghal as the spectral guard. We were left alone.

Bands of metal were woven, layer over layer to form the door. It was beautiful. As beautiful as it was I expected it held some very ugly traps within that weave.

I was not wrong, the door was equipped with many deadly and diabolical traps. It took us all to think through them and manipulate them within the puzzle that was the door of the devil lords home. We were lucky to suffer only two effects from the seven traps we encountered. Two razor sharp blades swung out from the left and right of the door. They swung in toward the center of the door and disappeared into the weave of the metal bands. It could have been my death if Fionaghal had not been there with lightening reflexes to pull me back. I still took a slice across my forehead that bled profusely. Andreas bandaged that wound. Later a blast of fire scorched us all and the smell of burnt flesh and hair filled the air. Fionaghal's reflexes saved us from more severe damage when she turned her armored back to the flame and shielded us from it.

We spent a great deal of time there dealing with all of that. No one came to interrupt. That was only a matter of time and added to our tension.

When we finally got beyond the door, a corridor curved away from us with the inner contours of the structure. To our left and right, arches opened into the blocks that made up the rooms of the structure at this level. To our right rooms had balconies that looked out over the plaza, to our left they looked out over the arena. The stage was just below. There were no occupants in any of those rooms.

The hall swept around the arena. When we came to the end of it we stood before another door of metal bands. What caution we had spent there had been unnecessary, although the door was trapped it was fixed to harm intruders who came from the other way. We had not been examining it for long when the door was unlocked and yanked open by another spectral guard. He was armed and armored as the other. We stepped back into the closed corridor, to draw him off of another colonnade.

He swung his cudgel down at me through the open door. Fionaghal reached over my head and stopped his arm. The guard looked up at her and I jumped to drive my blades through his neck and sever the spine. The implosion occurred and the armor clanged against the floor. We hesitated only long enough to check for any adversaries that would come to the sound of the implosion or the falling armor. None came and we moved onto the colonnade, closing the door behind us.

We ran along the colonnade to another door. It was a metal door too, but it was of plain construction. That had no bearing on the traps involved. A metal ball on a metal arm shot down out of the ceiling and hit Andreas in the back of the head. He went down like a sack of wheat. Fionaghal tended to him while I worked the door.

I removed the remaining traps with efficiency. They were beginning to repeat those I had already seen in the arena and in the necropolis. On the other side of the door was a landing, and stairs descended to the floor below. We had seen all of Devil's home.

Devil was not at home, but we did not know the full extent of his powers and wondered if he could keep himself hidden even from an angel of the heavenly host. We had not seen him in the plaza with the army that prepared there. He must have ventured out at last to command his armies on the field of battle with Man.

We moved midway down the stairs to another landing, with Andreas between us and leaning on me. He assured me he was alright. The unfocused look in his eyes said other wise.

From the landing we had a better view of our surroundings. The flight of stairs on which we stood to leave, faced those we had taken up into Devil's home. We moved down the stairs to a door we knew would lead back to the plaza. We wanted one more look before we took flight from the arena. We moved with stealth, but purpose was our priority.

We were wholly disappointed to find Devil away from home. Our already thin patience tattered and Andreas and I blamed each other for wasting the time and allowing them to slip away. I opened the door a crack and was surprised to find the plaza empty. In the distance, emitting from the many tunnels that led back to the necropolis, we could hear the hard drumming and chanting of Devil's dark army as they went to engage with the little army of Man.

We worked under the assumption that whatever the powers of the orb were they had figured them out and marched to unleash them upon the race of Man on Earth. A gift of God's goodness turned around to destroy his creation. Devil's revenge would be complete. If he could not destroy Earth, his great act would set us back hundreds of years into darkness. Enlightenment would seem a waste of time. Despair would rule the hearts and minds of the people. Hatred and greed would follow.

Our own hope was waning. To think we could best the devil at his game was at least arrogant; at the worst impossible.

Devil was out there somewhere. If Diony's small contingent of religious men and mystics were successful at sealing the veil the host would be turned back, Earth would be safe, Devil would be outraged at his continued exile, and we would be behind enemy lines. Our chances of making it back to a gate with the devil's armies spread throughout the nine levels of Hell were slim to none.

Our best chance of escape was to follow close behind the armies. Then we could make a break through the lines and return to our people and aid the fight against Devil and his annihilation of Man.

The fight was for freedom; the right to be at peace with ones self as well as with others. This was a fight for humanity; to find light and keep it.

We ran.

We fought when denizens of the necropolis tried to stop us. Fionaghal's fierceness and my expertise cut the enemy down while Andreas kept us protected and whole. I felt like we could take on any enemy together. It was likely that would be tested.

We ran.

We went up through the ossuary. The necromancer's henchmen were there. I knew how to best them this time and Fionaghal followed suit.

We ran through the rotunda. The wall of flames was up. We leaped through and ran, stumbling across the dark space until we came to the gate that would take us to the dark passages and up to the kettle lake within the flat topped hills.

We taught Fionaghal the rhythm to the gate key music and she played it out upon the rhythm sticks We played on flute and harp and the gate sprung open for us. We played it closed again, then we played it locked.

We ran up the stairs around the mephitic gas.

We ran up through the passages to the bridge that spanned the kettle lake. The village was a bustle of activity. The devils that lived there were beginning to mobilize. The dark army was taking on massive proportions. We could hear the drums and marching over the hills above us. The dark army from the necropolis was just ahead.

Fionaghal could fly us out of the kettle valley, but we had the opportunity to diminish Devil's reinforcements. We ran across the bridge before we were noticed and attacked a group loading wagons. The clash of battle soon brought others to the fight. Fionaghal and I went back to back with Andreas between us unloading all manner of elemental magic upon the horde and all manner of protection to envelope us. Panic ensued when Andreas blew dozens of them into the lake. The creature there was hungry. Those that survived to pull themselves from the water fled. We fought on and in the end we shredded that army. Any that were stupid enough to stay and fight fell before us.

The wagons held all manner of military gear. It pained us to leave it behind, but we would never get it up the mountain unseen by Devil's armies. We dumped it into the lake, wagons and all.

We ran again; over the hills to the red sand desert. We ran along the border between hills and desert, to the mountain.

We climbed.

The dark army was ahead of us. We skirted around the mountain stopping and hiding, moving and darting, up through the rocks to get ahead of the army. We pierced the black sky to enter the land of Malisgalar's lair.

It was tempting to escape via Ender Prison but that would bring us out too far from the pierce in the veil. Flying was not an option either; there were no other creatures in flight. If Devil was there he would surely order to have us shot down.

More armies merged at the foot of the mountain. Like busy ants they joined the other armies and swarmed toward us.

We were anxious to increase the distance between us and the armies and we climbed too quickly. Our movement gave us away. A call went up from the army below and a throng of hands went up to point us out. Dark arrows rained down, but Andreas got up a protective dome and the arrows bounced away. We were tired, and so many arrows fell that Andreas lost strength quickly.

Fionaghal risked all to take us up under her arms and leaped into the air. The strength of her bound took us to the shelf at the caves that would take us up out of the mountain and onto Earth in the land of Pyr.

Tourabain's little army of Pyritiums and Mareesians would not be enough for the army that was about to spill out of Hell and swallow them up.

We started out to warn them, but Fionaghal faltered. Her leap into the air surprised us. Andreas could not compensate his protective magic quickly enough and she was pierced by an arrow of Bane Metal. It already festered and her skin burnt black around it. Andreas cut it out and pushed down on it to force the tainted blood out. A quick rinse with water and we moved again.

We ran through the caverns. Fionaghal pushed on, but she did not look well. When we reached Tourabain's army she fell to the ground and physicians came to her aid.

We warned the old paladin, Tourabain, of his predicament. He had no countermeasure. Diony was seeking assistance from other sources, but there was not enough time. This was the army he had and no more.

Eble and Eli had been to the cave in an attempt to mend the veil between Earth and Hell. They could not mend what they could not see. They attempted to weave a veil of their own. Eble wove protective wards throughout the caves in hopes of damaging the approaching horde, but he was uncertain of their effectiveness against base evil. Eli performed holy rituals against evil and the Devil hoping to turn them back. Then they prayed together to make their individual rites as one seamless shield of faith. They prayed that shield would extend to the army of Man. We found them now on the front line of their little army, still praying.

Andreas and I took up places on the line between Eli and Eble and rested while we waited. Eli prayed aloud profusely. Eble concentrated on what protection he would provided during the initial contact.

We waited for hours and the swarm of dark horde did not come. Even their drums had gone silent. The light of day sank behind the grey atmosphere of Pyr's smoke and ash. We heard them then. They emerged slowly from the dark hole of the cave to spread out across the base of the mountain. Hours went by and they did not advance, but their line became more dense and spread out further to each flank. The moons rose in the sky but their light was subdued in the smoky atmosphere and gave no advantage.

There was no standard raised to announce the position of their lord, Devil.

Without shouted order or beat of drums they advanced in the middle of the night. They moved slowly toward us and stopped. A pause proceeded both ends of the line moving forward. When they stopped each column split again and half of them moved forward and stopped.

Our soldiers were growing anxious and their fear was tangible. I was certain that Devil was counting on that fear to feed his armies audacity.

The furthest armies suddenly turned and flowed into a flanking position then stopped again. Several moments of silence followed until they charged down on us. Arrows from the front line of Devil's horde rained down on us at the same time. Still no orders were shouted, no drum beats timed their moves.

Eble threw up a dome to protect us and Andreas blasted his elemental forces right behind it. When the first arrows hit they ricocheted and many of the dark army fell, pierced by their own arrows.

It was not enough to stop the advance on our flank, but the arrows stopped. Each hit of a weapon against Eble's shield weakened it and Eble strained to hold it.

"Bring it down!" Tourabain shouted. Eble did and the horde fell upon us. The fighting was immediately intense and gruesome, but we fought well and just when the horde was about to retreat and regroup Tourabain yelled, "Again, Eble!"

Eble threw up the shield. Some horde were crushed by it and died under the force. Others were trampled against it as their fellows pushed against them. Our little army killed the rest. Moral went up and we piled the bodies up along the inside rim of protection. It was a grizzly defense but we held. Our wounds were severe and we lost men in that assault, but the survivors stood up in brave defiance.

I wondered what Devil thought of us then.

We watched as the surprised army spread out to fill the strategic formation again. They did not know when Eble let down the dome so he could rest. We moved him back into our center and paired him with Andreas. Fionaghal rejoined and we walked together among the army and gave them praise and encouragement.

When the next attack came it came from three sides at once. Fionaghal and I were at a place where the left flanking army swung down from the advancing front. Flying beasts rose from their rear lines and flew over to probe the dome. When they realized it was down they banked, screeched, and then plunged down on us.

The flyers tormented us as the horde advanced. Tourabain, a captain from Mareese, and one from Pyritia fought to protect Eble and Andreas. When Eble had conjured his protection in the first attack

192

and the force of it had crushed the soldiers of Devil's army, it was a fortunate surprise to us. We quickly recognized its use as a weapon and we used it again.

When the horde was within ten feet of our lines Eble let it fall in a wide swathe on top of them. Thousands fell beneath the force. The remaining horde retreated. Our archers dispatched those flyers that had been caught in the dome and we reset to wait for Devil's next move.

Eble rested while Andreas expounded on the possibilities of what the two of them could do together. Eble listened and I could see that he was excited about the possibilities.

I stayed beside Fionaghal and again we spoke to our soldiers. When we were alone again she spoke to me, "We are doing well; minimizing their numbers, but I have not seen Devil yet. With the veil still open; this war will never be over if we do not eliminate him."

"He must be there. We fought the horde on Earth before. They were never this organized. They would have turned away from us already in search of weaker prey."

"We must find him."

"Are you suggesting that we leave here in search of him?"

"I am."

"As tempting as that seems I think it would be our death."

The look she gave me was incredulous. "You have your doubts, but have you forgotten how well we fought together?"

"No, but we had Andreas to support us."

She looked to where Andreas conferred with Tourabain and Eble. They were formulating a strategy. "He is needed here. We can fight our way to Devil together. When we find him he will be vulnerable to me. I am not held with his vile chains now and his necromancer is dead. They will not be able to leech my life from me.

God is the only one with the power to undo him forever. I will be his sword."

I looked back to Andreas.

"The dome is down now, Saeede. Devil's army is dismayed. The time is now."

I did not respond immediately. I looked once more toward Andreas, hoping that he would see me and know I was leaving. I had slipped away from him unannounced in our first foray into Hell. It was something I deeply regretted. He looked at me at last and I stared into his eyes, into his heart, and mind as we could do to each other. He stood as if to stop me, but then he placed his hand on his heart and nodded. I blew him a kiss. He caught it and held it to his heart. Tourabain and Eble paid him no mind as they considered the movement of troops drawn out in the dirt.

I turned back to Fionaghal. "Let's go then." I said.

She bowed to Andreas and we slipped away into the darkness at the rear of our left flank.

***

The smoky sky of Pyr fell to the ground with the heavy night air. The exposed moons and stars cast our shadows on the ground. We now had to compensate for the light. We swung wide of the Devil's army to hide shadow as well as body. The dark army regrouped, and when they stood in formation again we dashed to the mountain.

The mountain gave us cover among the rocks and trees. We were nearing the mountain cave when an arm rose up; silhouetted in the light of the moons. In that hand an orb. The orb caught the light and it shone with an azure light. The army of the devil charged at the army of Man. God's Eye was the standard of the devil's army! The silent command to attack! This could not stand.

Fionaghal reacted without a moment of hesitation. She leaped to the orb and snatched it out of the hoardling's hand—Jest's hand! I ran and tackled the little beast. We tumbled but I managed to straddle the demon and discovered that it was not Jest within my grasp. In one startled, shocking, moment I looked into eyes that I knew all too well—Lily. The *blue* eyes of Lily. Whether it was disguise or illusion I couldn't be sure, but with the meeting of our eyes it fell away all at once.

Lily- Gebha -Jest, the elusive assassin responsible for the death of an ambassador and a king was tight in my clutches.

We had captured her once, along with her duped uncle, the king of Breen, but she escaped. She killed her uncle and walked out through the forces of the Ahngesian kings. She and King Narhan disappeared and we never saw him again.

She had infiltrated an ambassador's entourage and fooled an entire city with her disguises. She had managed to convince the ambassador's chief protector to arrest my own mother for the crime. We fell for her elaborate ruse until she disappeared. Our pursuit of her took us on a chase across the sea., where she had duped a king to turn against his country and seek a war with neighboring kings. She had been in collusion with an enemy king. Now I wondered; who exactly was that king? The possibilities of who he could actually be seemed monumental now. Could he have been the shadowy figure Lily called Tempter? Was Tempter, another of Devil's minions? Perhaps Narhan was under some dark control by Tempter, or was Tempter another prince of Hell, named Malisgalar, my father? Was my father manipulating Lily and her position on Ahnges to get to me? Who ever she was their conspiracy pitted the neighboring kings against each other. Back then we thought that King Narhan and King

Harald had conspired against five of the other seven kings, but was it Lily and Tempter who conspired against all seven to claim the spoils, before anyone knew what happened? In the light of finding her here—a key player in Devil's schemes, perhaps she was even more than Lily, the assassin niece of an Ahngesian King. She had certainly managed to wrangle a way into Devil's inner circle. How far had she gone to get there?

All of these things flooded my mind. She must have used the orb in *all* of these things. It explained so much. She led us into all of these dangers. She allowed us to see her and follow. Then each time as we closed in she must have used the orb. We thought we were so clever and though she eluded us we had still saved the day. Had even that been part of the plan? When she did not resurface after a time we felt safe and began to forget about her. I was shocked. To have her in my grasp in that place at that moment was important. The idea that she could stand before us as Jest and not be recognized both alarmed and mystified me. I had not the time to reason out what it all meant. Those short seconds of racing thought caused me to hesitate and she went for a knife in her sleeve.

The flash of steel brought me back to my senses and I ran her through before she could finish her move. She did not die right off. I did not remove my blade, and I finished her off with a jerk and a twist that severed her organs. I looked her in the eye and watched the life go out of her. I imagined that if I did not, she might vanish like a vapor and reform into someone else. I had so many questions for her, but they were not to be answered.

I became angry. Despair followed close behind that. I wanted to beat my emotions out on her. The thought of beating a dead man— woman; was sick, even for me.

Fionaghal came beside me. She helped me to hide Lily-Gebha-Jest among the rocks, then we went to the cave.

Four skeletal guards stood only a few fotmal away from the entrance; their attention was on the battlefield. We did not falter in our steps and slipped into the cave behind them.

That maneuver nearly cost us all that we had come to accomplish. Devil must have sensed us, because he was ready for us. We became aware of him as he flung an unseen force that propelled us into the backs of the skeletal sentries just outside.

That commotion in turn got the attention of the rear echelon. Before we could untangle ourselves from the sentries beneath us we were set upon by a swarm of the Devil's officers. It did not take them long to beat us senseless and effectively helpless. Devil himself stood over me and kicked me in the head. I did not lose consciousness, but I was ill and made sure to vomit on his boots.

Fionaghal did not fare as well. They separated us. They threw her limp form against a wall of the cave and I was held up for Devil's inspection.

"I see now why Malisgalar so wanted you as an heir. You are strikingly beautiful; and strong; so strong, and cunning, smart, and tenacious. You just don't give up."

If Devil expected me to answer; I did not. "Just as well," he said. "He was soft and thought he could win your love."

"He didn't know what love is."

"Are you so sure? Do you think we do not love?"

"I know that you don't. If you did you would not seek to destroy us."

"You have it backwards little one. We were quite happy in our exile until you began to encroach and fight us back."

"Had you stayed in exile we wouldn't have had to 'encroach' We only fight because you contaminate our lives. You are insidious; feeding your evil on our doubts, crushing dreams with fear and apprehension."

"I admit I did take some pleasure in wronging a few rights. I wouldn't have if your god hadn't put me on this planet with you. I would have been perfectly happy serving out my exile alone, but you were all so appealing. I found you all amusing and I could not resist the temptation to manipulate you. You are a weak minded race, with few exceptions. I didn't even have to come out of my hole to do it. One seed planted telepathically in one mind and the rest just grew on its own; one weak mind to another."

He came close to me then, and reached out his hands as if to embrace me. I squirmed in the grasp of the two demons that held me, but they were strong and I was too weak.

He took my face in both hands and kissed me once on each cheek. "Take her to the front. Beat her until she cries for mercy, then bring her to me. If she does not, then kill her. Either way that should bring their army in to us. The angel is mine."

I knew he meant to kill Fionaghal, but even that awful realization was dulled by the expectation of my own pending death, by torture.

They dragged me toward the fighting. Three fighters fashioned a pillory in a tree a little removed from their camp. My armor was removed and passed on to any who wanted it. When the one who controlled me had my wrists tied and moved to tie my ankles, I slipped the ropes over his head and snapped his neck. As he fell I got a hold on his wide sword and ran before the others were aware of what happened.

I ran for cover in the rocks but my motion gave me away and the fighters pursued me. I had to fight. That was awkward with my hands still tied, but there were only three of them and I managed not to die before I killed them. They still managed to hurt me badly, but there was no time to tend my wounds.

My melee in the rocks had not gone unnoticed and I counted six more making their way to me. I used the rocks to my advantage and took positions where I could force several to reroute while I dealt with one or two at a time. I managed in this way to survive once again but I was nearing exhaustion.

I sat and held the blade upright between my knees and sawed through the ropes at my wrists.

I could see above the fighting from my vantage point on the mountain slope. I found Andreas among the leaders of the army in the command ring. They saw the pillory go up. They knew that we had been captured and that we would probably not survive what they had planned for us. The commanders of The Army of Man were growing frantic. The outcome of this battle did not look good for them.

As I watched the battle taking place below me I was attacked from behind. The first blow came from the flat side of my own scimitar. It was hard across my back. Air escaped my lungs and another blow, with my other scimitar, came hard across the back of my head. I fell forward, but rolled to face my attacker from the ground. The creature that leaped at me was so like a human that it seemed out of place among the horde.

I got my legs up and caught him in mid air. The air went out of him and I flipped him over my head. I jumped up, dizzy, but I leaped upon him anyway. We tangled in the rocks, rolling and sliding over them. Our blades hit us both several times until we gave up attempting to use them at all. We ended up in a rock slide that took us rolling down the slope. At the bottom we had our hands around each others' necks. Too tired to try anything else we could only squeeze and hope the other died first.

I was next aware of battle noises, but could not comprehend my situation at first. My adversary lay beside me. He was dead and I felt dead. I killed him only seconds before I lost consciousness and he fell off of me. Our fight had been lost in the mayhem of the main battle and though I remained unfound, I was certain my captors would be hunting for me. I crawled back up the slide of scrabble rock that had propelled us down hill. I needed weapons and searched for our dropped swords. I found one scimitar and the wide sword near the place where we had given them up. They had been partially buried along the spill. They were battered, but they were better than nothing.

I continued my crawl until I came near the cave behind the rear echelon. I could see the tree and it was empty. I scanned the troops for a sign of Devil but he was nowhere to be seen. He had to be in that cave with Fionaghal. My spirit sank. I had been away from her for a long time. I did not know how long I had lain unconscious. I had little hope of finding Fionaghal still alive.

The dark army had gained ground and was moving forward as the battle ensued. I could see the dark carcasses lying across the field in heaps around the camp of the mortal army. I made my way to the cave undetected and slipped in.

I was amazed by what I saw and rejoiced that I had arrived in time. At the far end Fionaghal had Devil backed into a corner. She killed him with a bolt of blue lightning that she wielded like a sword.

The lightening exploded in Devil's chest and Fionaghal was thrown against a wall. The explosion lifted me and put me on the ground outside of the cave. Still stunned, I got to me feet and went to Fionaghal.

She was alive and conscious, but exhausted. It was easy to see that she had fought desperately with Devil. She suffered many cuts and was bleeding badly. One cheek was badly bruised and the eye was swollen shut. When I got her to her feet she could not straighten up. Some unseen wound caused her great pain, but still she insisted on confirming Devil's death. She went to look over the body of Devil. She dripped some of her own blood down his throat. Smoke billowed from his mouth and he sank in on himself. He looked like a corpse that had lain in the sun to dry and blacken.

Fionaghal said a prayer over Devil's body and I guarded her as she did. When she was ready we exited the cave.

We were tired, but Devil's death emboldened us. I gave Fionaghal one of my swords and we engaged the rear of the dark army. Fionaghal fought, but she was hunched over from her internal pain. I looked for Andreas. He saw us and began a fevered assault in our direction. He had a long way to come and unrelenting horde to wade through.

Our rear attack confused the officers there and we were able to destroy several before they recovered. Their best warriors had been held back from the battle. They were ordered to engage with us. If the sheer number of the black armies was not enough to destroy the puny army of Man then these elite forces would go in and finish them.

Fionaghal and I would not survive that battle We were vastly outnumbered and too close to exhaustion to fight well. We fought just to take out as many of them as we could and give the puny army of Man another chance at survival.

They attacked us with a fierceness I could not defend. I fell quickly. My attackers fell on me as I lay upon the ground. I knew my death or something worse was at hand and that it would be excruciating. I struggled against them with the remnants of my strength. There were just too many and my struggles were useless. Fionaghal still fought, but many of those who had been on me turned to her.

Two of the elite warriors took charge of me and beat me just for fun. I fell to the ground and they kicked me relentlessly. I protected myself the best I could with my arms over my head and my legs up to my chest. They concentrated their blows at my head anyway. My head spun and my focus failed. The fun went out of it then for my attackers. I felt myself being hoisted up by arms and legs. They tied me by my feet to the trunk of the pillory tree and my hands were tied to a thick branch above my head and out in front of me. My body sagged and the pressure on my shoulders and lower back was nearly unbearable.

I raised my head to look around and found myself facing the field of battle. Those who opposed the devil would see the beating. Andreas saw me. The realization of what he saw made him frantic. He tried to get through the thick of the battle. I watched in anguish as he, Tourabain, and a captain fought a losing battle to get to me. The main battle was going just as badly. I could not see Eble on the field at all and assumed he had fallen. The battle between light and dark was now a primal fight between two forces. With Devil, Malisgalar, the necromancer, Jest, Eble, and Fionaghal gone and Andreas's elemental powers spent—no magic came to the aid of either side.

The two who had me, bragged about how proud Devil would be of them when they threw me at his feet to beg for mercy. A punch to my jaw knocked me out preventing me from telling them he was dead.

When I came to again I was dripping with foul smelling water. Reality flooded back and I struggled against my binds; to no avail.

I looked up, fearful of what I would see of the battle. The dark armies had the army of Man in a fighting retreat. We were lost. My heart ached for Man.

As soon as my captors knew I was awake a rapid series of stones were thrown to hit my back and sides. The horde around me cheered and called for more. Their request was obliged quickly. My body was so weak that I couldn't cry out against the pain.

An executioner came around to face me. He held several thin blades in both hands. He met my eyes and smiled. "You will cry out before I am done with you. You will be an example to any of the humans who survive. Because of you they will learn to comply." He ran one of the blades across my chest and caught the blood in a crystal bowl. I didn't want to think about what ritual they had in store for me.

I would not give him the satisfaction of crying out. I clamped my teeth together and set my jaw against the pain. I did not break eye contact even when he sliced me three more times. I shook with shock and weakness. The executioner laughed.

I could not find the anger to call up the growl and fling my tormentors away from me, though I tried. I was too far gone, too weak. My mind was surrendering to the pain; to the hopelessness of our fight against evil.

He jabbed me two more times, once through each bicep. I clung to consciousness, but I had no fight for it and I slipped into blackness.

The clang of battle came to me again in waves, but it was the beating of rocks and clubs against my ribs that brought me to reality. I prayed for death to take me, until it stopped.

I opened my eyes. I was out of focus. Two demons came up very close to look into my eyes. They wanted to be sure I was aware, before taking turns hitting me with their fists They challenged each other and each hit came harder than the last. I felt bones snapping, I reached for the darkness and welcomed it when it came, but it was fleeting.

More foul water was thrown up into my face and filled my mouth and sinuses. I choked. The pain that caused confirmed that I had broken ribs. I ventured a look for Andreas, but I could not find him. More foul water was tossed onto the open knife wounds . That searing pain was far worse than any they had delivered onto me so far. I could not contain the cry that rose out of me.

"Call for mercy and this can end." The voice of my torturer, my executioner, was like a whisper in a dream. I felt myself weaken. I wanted to give in. To die would have been a comfort. "Cry mercy," he said, "and it will be yours."

I looked over his head to the field of battle. Eli and Tourabain were with Andreas. They had gathered forces to them and were spearheading an advance and cutting the devil's line in half. There was little hope for victory, but they would not surrender to evil, for the sake of humanity. Neither could I.

"If only I could." My voice was weak and dry. I sounded like I was somewhere nearby, not inside myself. I struggled against my binds but that only tightened them. The wounds on my wrists from the chains of Devil's prison reopened and blood dripped down my arms to join with the blood from the knife wounds. It all converged to drip from my belly onto the mud below me. Carrion birds began to circle over head.

"As you wish, Hu-man." The words came and more stones were thrown at me.

The executioner laughed.

The flats of my own swords were beaten against my ribs and I could feel more bone give beneath them. My breath was strained and ragged. I shook uncontrollably now, but I fought for consciousness. I wanted to see the battle. I wanted to die with the army of Man.

The front line of the devil's army split and the advantage went to the army of Man. They fought with valor and they gained ground until Devil's elite emerged from hiding among the rocks and trees. They swarmed down off the rise at the base of the mountain. The army of Man faltered, but under Tourabain's orders braced for the fight.

I gave up at that moment. Fionaghal had killed Devil but his armies fought on to advance his agenda. For all I knew they had killed her too and then rejoined the fight. If Devil's army had learned of their lord's demise, it inspired them. They fought on with a relentless fury. If I called for mercy, perhaps I could bargain with my captors. Maybe I could buy the Army of Man some time; time to win, or time to escape; whatever the outcome—I had to try to save them. I would give myself to the dark army and save the army of Man—save Andreas. I only hoped that they would accept me as ransom. I would bargain my life for the freedom of Man. Once man was safe I would let myself die. I could bear that. I would even bear being enslaved to them if Man were at peace; free from Devil's influences. Whatever the price, it would be worth it if they would treaty to return to their underworld and leave Mankind alone. I knew it sounded so naive, but I had to try.

The word came to my mind—*"mercy."* It never passed my lips. A profound stupor hit me like a bad drug.

At the same moment a wall of blue flame came down in a circle between the armies. My heart cheered for Andreas and his elements. Behind the wall those demons that were trapped on the side of Man fell quickly to their angry blades.

The demons cheered, thinking that Devil had dropped the wall. They felt confident that they could pass through. Hundreds died trying. The confused hoardlings fell back but managed to regroup.

Andreas stood at the edge of the ring of fire. His arms were outstretched to his sides and his head was thrown back. I had seen this position many times before and knew he was preparing to channel more elemental power. His arms came forward and his hands clapped, but nothing happened. The flames remained and no other effect occurred. He tried again and nothing.

My fight for consciousness failed and I swooned into the ether of death.

·~·Chapter Sixteen·~·

The sounds of battle came to me even in that overwhelming collapse. Awful screams went up in the clash of the combat. Then I fell through a long silence, until I felt and heard a great rumble. Then silence again. I tried desperately to open my eyes, but I could not. I would go to my death without knowing the victor.

I was about to die on the threshold of Hell. I was terrified. What chance at Heaven could I have so close to Devil's minions. They would not make my eternal death a peaceful one and Heaven barely knew me, if at all.

I felt a sensation like falling, but my thoughts faded and left me, as if I had prayed myself to sleep. I knew nothing more and slept for what seemed like a long time, until I heard voices; soft comforting voices. I tried and this time my eyes opened.

I was lying on the ground. Massive white pillars supported a white ceiling above me.

I remembered what had caused my death, but found no pain remaining from the torture. There were no bandages. Small scars were all that indicated I had ever been cut. Surely then, I was dead.

I sat up and discovered that I was at one end of a vast pavilion. At the opposite end there was a gathering of men. I stood to go to them. They noticed and they all turned to look at me. One came forward with an arm outstretched in greeting. Under the other arm he carried a great tome sealed with many great locks. I wondered at what a tome in such a place could be, but I feared I was not worthy to know so I did not ask.

Then I looked, and saw that behind this man was a great throne. Seven braziers lit the area and I could see twenty four old men surrounding the throne. Around the pavilion were all types of living beasts. Some like to those I had seen in Hell. Four were full of eyes that could see everywhere at once. Then I felt a touch on my arm; an angel's touch —Fionaghal's touch. In her other hand was God's Iris. She urged me forward and walked beside me.

"So, Heaven then." I thought to myself.

Fionaghal smiled and nodded.

My steps faltered. I was afraid to move upon the hallowed ground of Heaven.

"Be not afraid, Saeede. They are here for you; to greet you."

"Then it is true that I have died?"

"Not yet." She said no more, but took my hand and led me forward.

The man with the outstretched hand received the Iris from Fionaghal and draped his arm around my shoulder to draw me close. He met my eyes. "I am the son," he said. "You are truly as a sister to me."

I was dumbfounded. I could not speak and he smiled his understanding of my condition.

He led me to the throne.

Upon the throne was the most beautiful man I had ever seen. He was a perfect blend of all that was beautiful in every race of Man. Even as I looked on his beauty I could see that in him roiled the stars and moons. I saw in him the cosmos as Fionaghal had described it.

He stood and came down the dais to stand before me. "Do not fear us, Saeede. We are grateful to you. It is not often a mortal comes to the aid of the heavenly host unbidden. I owed you protection, though you never sought it for yourself; only for others.

"Devil and I struggled across the cosmos, in worlds that run in the ether around yours. When I overpowered him at last, your world was the one best suited to cast him down from Heaven. Devil was cunning and powerful and with angels of his own; what you call demons and hoard-lings. He soon had a civilized realm much like this, but his was intent on evil, while I sought a way to nourish my creations. I wanted peace for them.

"The holy angels are strong of body and mind and yet they choose to obey me absolutely. I have much use for them. They are swift and as elusive as the wind. They are loyal to me and to the tasks and charges that I assign them. Fionaghal has had hands full caring for you. I am as thankful for her as I am for you.

"Even when we could not protect you from your father you fought back with goodness and regard for all Mankind. Even before you knew Fionaghal and after you knew her to be an angel you still took all things upon yourself; even to the point of sacrificing yourself for the sake of Man. This I could not allow.

"Now you lie on the threshold of death. You have a choice. You can come to us here and give up worldly things, or you can go back and have your life. Devil will bother you no more. He is bound in death and his spell is broken. Many who were lost to him are free now and wander in search of their lost lives and loved ones. His angels have fallen and their deaths will be punishment for them. Peace will be yours at last either way you choose."

I only stared at Him. I had not even considered Him until recently and now He stood before me and thanked me. He offered a peace that most people could only dream of and not fully understand.

He knew my thoughts and spoke again.

"Your faith is something pure, if somewhat unguided. You came to me of your own accord. It took time and a dark existence. I always hoped you would come and play the part I had chosen for you. You have done well in the face of evil; mortals usually succumb. You did not, for this I am happy and grateful.

Usually a reward for a mortal is a subtle answer to a prayer, but for you I grant you once to be able to choose and I will grant it. Life or death—Earth or Heaven."

Still I gazed on Him and did not speak. God spoke to me in the present. He was in a form I could understand, not some vague thing. I wondered if His beauty would be the same to others as it was to me, or would we all choose to see Him in our own way.

Knowing my thoughts he spoke again.

"I am the center of that boundless collision of energy that you call the titan's blast. You, and all the planets of the universe spun off of that great moment of miraculous creation. I remained at the center. I am the beginning. I am the light and dark of it. I am that explosion. In that birth I knew all of creation and I nurtured it and formed it. It was me, and I, it. I am the universe and it is me. I am the sky and water; earth and stars. I am all around you and you live in me. I appear now for your comfort, but I could as easily present to you in my true form. Would you like to know me in that way?"

How could I say no? I did not speak it, but He knew.

Then I was alone. There was no ground beneath me or sky above. I was suspended in a magnificent space. I could make out stars and planets with moons and without. I tried to make out which one was my Earth. Gas and stars formed into vast clusters of colorful light that I had never seen and could not name. In those clusters I could see the face of God.

I had never known such awe. I had never imagined that such a thing could be possible. Thing—this is not adequate; there is no word adequate to describe what I saw.

His voice came to me from all around "Now you know me as I truly am. You know that I am real. I can grant you your life on your Earth or life with the angels in Heaven."

"Can I be an angel?"

I felt the universe heave and heard God sigh. "No," He said, with a depth of sadness I do not believe a mortal could withstand.

"All creation began in the moment that I became. The angels were like a shower of sparks at the beginning. They are myriad. It took man a great deal longer, there was much I had to do to all the earths to make species that could survive the planet. Angels came from the stuff of cosmos. You are from the stuff of Earth."

"Then I choose life on Earth. I finally have one that makes me happy—one that makes others happy. I can still do good on Earth."

"I am glad. You have chosen as I hoped. Your world may need you as much now as they ever did before. They will try to understand what has happened, your experience can help them with that. You already have that life. I want to give you something more.

In the far reaches of the universe in a cluster of stars and gas I witnessed an explosion followed soon after by another. Then a deep red orb the size of a large gem appeared in a nebula before me.

"Take it," He said, "It is the greatest prize that I can give you—for now. Perhaps you can be an angel, of sorts. When there is something that needs your touch I will call on you through the orb. There are many worlds that need a loving hand."

The speaking of those words was the last thing I remember of my time with God.

I was suddenly aware of my body being lowered from the pillory.

I could hear Andreas, "No! No, no no!" He shouted.

Eli came and prayed over me while someone wrapped me with a blanket.

Andreas raged. "God. Why this? Not her God, please!"

I drew breath and all speaking ceased.

I felt Andreas fall to his knees and take me up in his arms.

I opened my eyes and looked into his. The joy I saw there was worth the torture I had taken to the threshold between life and death. He pulled me close and we cried unashamed tears of joy.

When they helped me to my feet a red orb rolled out from under the blanket.

Andreas stooped to pick it up. He held it toward me, but could not take his eyes from it.

"That's mine," I said.

He did not dispute me and placed it into my shaking hand. "The Eye?"

"Not, The Eye, that has been returned. This is—the heart."

He met my gaze and knew there was more to tell. I knew that he would wait until I was ready.

He helped me back to the camp of Man's army. As we walked I could feel my strength returning. We were provided with a tent and spent the night sleeping in each others arms.

·~·Chapter Seventeen·~·

The next morning I was gifted a new set of armor and my repaired scimitars were returned to me.

We returned to the field of battle to oversee the recovery of the fallen. Great fires burned the dead of Hell's Army. The body of Lily Gebha Jest was burned with the rest. Her belongings were placed in a locked chest and sent ahead to be placed in our berth on Night's Angel.

Men were anointed. We lost Eble in the battle. Eli and I saw to him personally. Diony would mourn the loss of a dear friend and mentor as I already did.

The fallen soldiers of Crystalier were sent by horse and wagon to the Night's Angel. More wagons took the soldiers of Pyr into Pyritium. We followed them as a sign of respect and stayed for their service of mourning before returning to the ship.

Andreas, Eli, Tourabain, and myself marched ahead of what remained of the Army of Man. We could hear the men talking of angels that pulled them from the battle just as the wall of fire fell. Those that never believed before professed homage to a god who could do such things. Those who were already men of faith professed even more.

At the dock, shrouded bodies were being lifted carefully from the dock to the ship's hold. Captain Night's had the hard task well in hand. It was not long after we boarded, that he and his crew were preparing the ship for the voyage. Tourabain dealt with the dock master and Andreas and I kept our mouths shut about the ship we had stolen there until we were comfortably situated in our cabin.

"We really need to make good on that boat we stole."

"We will. Let's get you home first."

"Are we in time for the treaty talks?"

"Barely, but we'll make it."

We went through the box of Lily's things then. There were three vials of liquid. The knife that she had intended to kill me with was there, and coated with poison. A small sack packed with actor's makeup, small vials of hair, and glues to adhere them. Her disguise kit, so it was no black magic illusion that hid her identities, just a master's skill at disguise. There was also a finely crafted glassy black chain.

All of those things, as important as they were, were nothing compared to two scrolls that were among them.

The scrolls were a diary. They were written in almost daily, beginning shortly after her escape from the prison cart of The Five King's Army.

What we read boiled down to one thing: my father's desire to control me and take me as the beneficiary to his Hell. Two plots were launched against us at the same time. One by Devil to unlock the Hell Gates, the other by my father to compel me. My father, Malisgalar was favored by Devil. When Malisgalar went to Devil for assistance; the two plots became as one.

In the scrolls she laid it out in detail, just as we thought it had happened. When the first plot failed another more insidious plot took its place. We were played in both of them and didn't even know it.

Lily detailed the ill-concieved plan to overthrow The Ahngesian Kings. She realized when we bested her in Mareese that their arrogance had gotten the best of them. They also had not counted on King Frahn's humble call for peace and unity catching hold among Kings with a history of dissension. They did not count on us infiltrating Breen and capturing her or finishing the job by taking down their king.

We knew now that Lily had obtained the orb before Eindal's murder, when Fionaghal lost it protecting us from Devil's minions. She worked under orders from Devil himself, but on my father's behalf. She became Jest and built that hovel in the alley of Koman City.

I had been so sure that Jest was just Jest. I had suspected he was not and still she fooled me. I was physically repulsed by my own stupidity and regret.

She watched at the asylum gates when demons and devils began to emerge and knew that they had been sent out in search of us. She had no need to hide herself from them and fell in with them as who she really was—Lily. She was known to them as one favored by Devil. She was looked to as a leader.

At that same time the search for the scrolls was already on-going. Their man, Polqutius was failing to obtain them. When Malisgalar asked Devil for permission to bring his mortal daughter to Hell as an heir the two plots became one. Andreas and I had a reputation that was not unknown to my father. If they could get us to obtain the scrolls, then get me to turn against Andreas and deliver the scrolls to them; they would have all that they wanted. It was Lily's job to bring events together. She had been one of Devil's soldiers—a spy for a long time. Not simply the opportunist we had imagined. Lily tried many times to steer us toward Hell, but Fionghal fought to thwart that.

She hadn't counted on my guardian angel. Her notes detailed her encounters with Fionaghal. She knew Fionaghal was not human and soon began to call her simply, Angel. When Fionaghal began arriving each time Lily tried to way lay us she knew there was a connection. She only thought Fionaghal had been sent to thwart Devil's plans to unlock the gates. She knew she would have to be very cunning. It was clear she did not know who she was to me.

Fionaghal wore the orb on a gold chain and kept it tucked into the gold sash she wore around her torso. In the chaos of battle the chain broke and the orb fell free. Lily saw this from her place of command and waded through battle to retrieve it for herself. When the angel fell in that battle and did not disappear as she had always done; Lily had a pretty good idea that vanishing was a power of the orb. When she told Devil, he was furious that they had left the angel behind. He knew immediately that Fionaghal was a guardian angel, and most likely; mine. His final decision to return my father to life was based on that possibility.

Lily did not tell Devil about the orb.

The next time Lily saw Fionaghal, was in the battle near the asylum gate When Fionaghal fell there Lily saw an opprotunity to be rid of her. She used the orb to take her to the plaza of the necropolis and then hurried to see Devil and report. He sent his soldiers to search the battleground with orders to bring the angel directly to him. As a reward he gave her a shiny black chain necklace and placed it around her neck. She must have known what it was, but she often mentioned how proud she was to have been given that gift by her lord and not be affected by it.

I wondered aloud, "Was it the Bane Metal around her neck or all the lies and trickery that drove her mad enough to do so much evil on people?"

"Perhaps both. Still she must have had an amazing mind to overcome the full effects."

"Or, her necklace is not the same. I wonder... ," I said and took it out of the box. I could touch Bane Metal but was this that? "Would you be willing to touch it?"

He reached a tentative hand toward it and said, "Have you ever wondered if someone could become so insane as to become evil because of it?"

"I have actually. Its hard to think otherwise now."

Andreas touched one finger lightly to the chain and drew back, but then touched it again, and again, and then took it from me.

"Nothing."

"Some ingredient missing at the forging of the metal—blood of the insane."

"So, Devil actually cared about Lily?"

"It would seem so." I said.

We returned to the scrolls.

When she met Eindal near the gates of the asylum on Koman she attempted to throw him off of his quest for the scrolls by enticing him with a false story about the orb. He logged her half truths into his ledger and went on his way. When he could not withstand the Bane Metal at the asylum gates he turned back to Behlanna.

If Eindal knew my true nature at that time, he did not mention it in his ledger. Perhaps he did know and that is why he sought us. His decision not to write that would have been to protect me. I regretted again that we had not known the man.

The Mage Academy was the first one of Lily's plots that put us on the path she was steering us to. The ambush by bandits on the road to Behlanna was another. That caused us to choose to go to Behlanna for rest. Eindal was already there and Lily knew that he searched for us to aid him in his search for the scrolls. That is where Lily killed him for his ledger and one scroll while he sat on the porch of Aunt Kate's Boarding house in Behlanna. She took the ledger and planted it so that we would find it. Eindal's murder became the catalyst that put us where they wanted us.

Whether it was sinister intervention or extreme circumstance, events unfolded that put us in the thick of Eindals' murder investigation. The existence of Hell Gates and the plot to unlock them became known to us and our quest for the Gate Scrolls began.

We knew nothing about the orb or Fionaghal at that time so we did not know to search for them.

The death of one of Hell's princes did not go unnoticed. Soon Devil's necromancer was busy renewing the life force of my father. Lily noted that the ossuary was emptied to leech the souls needed to reclaim his black heart.

It took a year, but Lily and the Devil managed to regroup. During that time my father was in the care of the necromancer. He was too weak to take over as Narhan, but Lily was given a necklace of Argentium, Bane Metal to give to him as a token of her supposed esteem. He lost his mind quickly and it was Lily who controlled him at the beginning.

Lily expertly assassinated Esporanza and just as expertly left enough evidence to put us on the trail of the guard she was portraying. We chased the guard to Ahnges and it was there that we discovered the guard was actually Lily. We captured her and brought her to King Frahn for questioning. She was being transferred to Calibe for imprisonment when Soldiers of Breen ambushed her escort and rescued her. She went to Yer to hide and was there when we went to seek Narhan's compliance with the treaty conference. She had Narhan send us away. It is after this that she writes about Tempter.

She calls him Devil's messenger. Narhan has gone mad, and having no use of him, Tempter kills him and takes on his appearance. He is fierce and has the ability to cast her into a dream like state where she has no control of herself. Lily was much afraid of him. I was more convinced than ever that he was my father. His timing was bad though, had he eliminated Narhan earlier he might have been present when we went there to seek his agreement to Frahn's treaty conference.

Lily had been frustrated when Devil first gave her to him. She was the niece of King Breen and Tempter was working his own evils on Ahnges. Her uncle, was the weakest mind of the seven kings, but Narhan had been the most insidious. Tempter needed Lily to keep her uncle on plan. It was easy to do.

When Ambassador Esporanza was assigned to go to Mareese, Lily agreed to the plan to assassinate him. That brought us back into play. Tempter was delighted.

Devil knew my father wanted me under his control. As Lily wrote it, Devil loved my father and contrived the means of bringing me back to Hell as a gift to him. Thanks to Lily's place in the house of Breen he knew of Frahn's plans to unify Ahnges and to send an ambassador to Mareese to forge a trade agreement. The plan was launched to place Lily in the ambassador's entourage.

When things turned against them with the Ahngesian Kings and Lily was captured it was too late to swing events back into their favor. Tempter was gone and Lily was left alone. She returned to the necropolis and pleaded for another chance.

Devil was growing impatient with Lily's failures. And Malisgalar was furious. Lily knew then that Tempter and my father were the same. It was then that she revealed the orb to Devil, saying only that it gave her the power to vanish and that she had obtained it at the Mage Academy. She knew she lied to the devil, but gaining a higher seat in his hierarchy was more important to her even than her own life. She considered herself lucky that he still trusted her and did not put her words to a test.

It was Malisgalar who concocted the magic that would draw Fionaghal's spirit out and draw me to her. I tried to deny that had worked. I wanted to believe it was Eindal's ledger and God's Eye in the hands of evil that brought me in. That and that alone. Else why did I not feel the pull on me before I heard of the angel? Still, there were the circumstances that Fionaghal had manipulated, and those of God and Devil, Lily, and even my father. It grieved me to realize that I had been such a pawn in Devil's game. It grieved me even more that people I cared for had been made pawns too.

It was becoming very clear that our experience at solving ordinary crimes did not translate when solving crimes committed against mortals by evil spirits. So much of what had happened to us was at the whim of god's and devils in a reality that even now was beyond my capacity to fully understand.

If God intended to use us for such things again, I hoped he instilled God's Heart with intuition.

The scrolls and the notes she had hidden in the depository in Breen were all recorded as a means of learning the ways of the hierarchy of Hell and to find a way into its highest command.

To us they were confirmation of the true purpose of the asylum and the necromancers activities there. She referenced the metallurgy recipes for Bane Metal and Blood Metal and how those tools worked to provide the necromancer with the fodder he needed to grow Devil's army of undead citizens.

Devil was dead. Malisgalar was dead. Lily's notes would tell us who the leaders of the nine levels were, and who would take two vacant seats Devil was their king and he had no heirs. Once the remaining leaders were dealt with and all gates and portals ultimately destroyed our earth could slowly return to peace.

Our work was not done, but it had to wait. We were on our way to Mareese for funerals and treaty talks.

·~·Chapter Eighteen·~·

We sailed on choppy seas through late spring storms. I had no root to quell my sea sickness. For only a brief moment I wondered why I did not need it. Stranger things had gone unexplained before. I decided to put this in the category of fortune.

On our second day out I took Andreas up to the prow and as we watched the world go by I told him about my experience in Heaven. We both looked at life very differently after that. We took the next days to help each other sort out all that we had suffered. When we returned to Mareese we felt mostly normal again.

Diony met us at the docks, accompanied as always by her man and Lord Protector, Brynal. She was happy to see us, and ecstatic that she had not had to deploy troops from any of the kings who were coming to Mareese for the treaty conference. Only the people of Crystalier and Pyr had been involved directly.

"I don't know how you did it, but you never cease to amaze me. Of course it was amazing that it was you, who somehow managed to stir up the trouble."

She was still annoyed at us for getting her involved. I could understand, but I wondered how she would feel if she knew I held the key to the universe in my pocket.

We returned to our apartment and composed a letter to Pinkert in Breen. We needed him to choose excellent soldiers for a special mission. With the information contained in Lily's journals we were confident that with the right support they could seek out and seal any of the portals hidden in Pyr, Ender Prison in Crystalier, or the Asylum on

Koman. Another letter went to Kapit in Behlanna. He had connections into places we could only imagine. We knew he would choose rightly. We had need of paladins, so one last letter went to King Dune. We spoke with Eli in hopes that he would go along as a way to continue his studies and to protect our men from uncertain evil. If he was interested when he returned we had need of a historian. He was anxious to be part of the mission and excited to have a part in the city of Breen. He made his arrangements at the academy.

Next we went to see Mam and Mya. We were interested to know if she could tell us the ingredients of the liquids we found in Lily's things. We visited for a time before showing her the vials. That they belonged to Lily was all we told her at that time. She tried to read more by looking me straight in the eye for a long time. I held her gaze and hoped she didn't see what I wasn't ready to tell her. She took the vials and went to her little workshop in a small room of the tower.

It took her a long time, but we spent it with Mya and enjoyed her very much. She had changed and was no longer the spoiled lost orphan of Ambassador Esporanza. We asked about her life and she shared her stories with zeal. We laughed for the first time in a long time and it was like an epiphany; suddenly our reality seemed normal again.

Mam returned with her findings. There were three vials of liquid and each was different. One was a strong paralyzing poison. Clear and tasteless it could have easily been put in food or drink.

I silently rejoiced that we had not let Lily Jest Gebha guide us to the asylum. I was sure she would have found a way to use it then. She would have taken me to my father then and neither of us would have been able to stop her.

Another was medicinal. Mam wrote that if she had mixed it she would have prescribed it to combat seizures. It seemed Lily was suffering from Devil's influence after all.

The last was oil of cotton seed and used to depress a woman's cycle. When Lily posed as a man it might have been difficult to hide the effects of menses. The oil was a necessary tool. Of all the side effects the most interesting was the depletion of melanin in the iris. Eye color depends on how much melanin you have in your iris. The more of the pigment you have, the darker the iris will be. Blue eyes have less than brown eyes, but grey eyes have even less. It explained why Jest's eyes were grey and not blue.

That was the last thing that nagged at my mind. I had been beating myself up about missing Jest as Lily. I had been right, but then on seeing him again I was convinced I was wrong. It was the grey eyes that were the final thing to sway me. It did little to alleviate my frustration on that point, but I resolved myself to enjoy the rest of the evening with Mam and Mya.

In the next few days we attended many funerals. The cost that our actions had taken weighed heavily. Eli consoled us. He pointed out that the cost to mankind would have been much more dire had we not acted. It was only a matter of time before evil would have marched forth from weakened gates.

Weeks went by while we adjusted to all that had transpired. We rested as much as we could. The Ahngesian kings arrived and the treaty talks went well. We went along on the tour of Mareesian artisans. The kings were impressed and arrangements were made for them to go on to the city of Jour. The treaty was all but finalized before they made that leg of their trip. We saw no need to delay further. We knew what products Jour had to offer and what Breen could trade in return. We asked Brynal to be our agent and gave him exact instructions as to what we would and would not sign on the treaty.

We made arrangements to move Mam, Mya, and their things to the ship. Andreas made arrangements to maintain our apartment in town permanently. When all was ready we went to our cabin on The Night's

Angel. I couldn't resist telling Captain Nights that only the angels of retribution have wings. I ventured a query. Since he was our captain and the ship was at our disposal, would he consider a name change?

"To what?" he asked.

"The Retribution. I have a feeling there will come a time when we sail her again that retribution will be our goal."

"I like it. I like it a lot."

"I'll help you paint."

***

We were back in Breen before the summer was over.

Pinkert had arranged beds in the attic of the stables. It was a fine barracks. Pinkert's select men were housed there and Kapit's rogues and Dune's paladins had already joined them. The stable master now had a room with the staff inside the fortress. When Eli arrived he chose to be housed with the men. We met with them as soon as we arrived and explained the mission in full. They were to go first to Koman where we knew the portal location. From Koman they would sail to Crystalier and using information we gave them they would seek the portal there and destroy it. Then on to Pyr where they would have to search without any help from us. Everywhere their mission took them they were to tend to the poor souls who could be saved, but if they could not be then our soldiers had to be prepared to destroy them. No evil could remain to taunt us again. They were ready and Night's sailed them the next morning.

We spent a few busy days getting Mam and Mya settled in at the fortress. It was wonderful. I found myself watching them often. My heart swelled with love for them.

Mya had matured during her time with Mam. She had a new confidence. She had learned grace and shared it often. She made friends

224

easily in town and among the household. She cared well for Mam and I thanked her for it. She made me proud to have her as a foster.

My Mam, who was often shunned for her unorthodox thinking, loved openly and without measure, it was impossible not to love her.

We told them our story piece by piece over the days. We knew it would take time for Mam to process all that we had been through. She nearly fainted when we told her of my torture at the hands of Devil's minions. Mam spanned every emotion and hugged us both often.

It was good to be with family; good to finally have a home, and what a home it was. Breen sat upon cliffs over the sea in a lush land good for lumber and crops, as well as fishing and hunting. Life was good.

Our home coming had not been without interest. Pinkert had to call upon the towns carpenters and seamstresses to make enough beds to outfit the new barracks. The arrival of rogues and paladins to support our own soldiers had people on edge. When Mam and Mya arrived at last there was curiosity about the queen's mother and foster.

Word of our return got around quickly and the people wanted to hear about our great adventure to save the world. At first the household workers dropped hints but when we weren't forthcoming they asked directly, and more often.

It all seemed so fantastic that we were sure they wouldn't believe us, but we invited Pinkert, Eli, and our valet, Enot, with his wife, Otta to hear our story first in private. Otta had become ripe with child in our absence and although she was uncomfortable she listened eagerly to every word. Enot doted on his wife, but listened well. Pinkert and Eli both jotted notes with pen and ink. The story was witnessed and properly recorded for history.

A few days later we told the story again at a banquet in the garden. Everyone was invited and it was standing room only. All of the Ahngesian rulers came and we told our story for all to hear. We did not embellish as is sometimes our habit. A story told at a king's table or in the corner of a pub must be captivating. We were sure this story could stand alone. When it came to the part about Heaven we left out the gift of the red orb—God's Heart. It was too precious a thing to reveal, and my greatest prize. We only told of my choice between life and death.

It did not take long for the story to grow. It was unfortunate, but legends have a life of their own and like it not we had stepped into that status.

***

A few weeks later an old man came to the gate. He claimed to be Maine, a young man who had gone missing after the death of his old parents only months apart. Maine had been missing for two years and should have been no more than twenty years old. The guards brought him to the fortress and we met with him in a room beside the garden.

We listened to his story. He had been saved by our special troop of men. We knew him to be a man who was turned demon by evil and Devil's encouragement. He told us things about his life in Breen before he turned to unprincipled ways and left.

We sent him out under guard and called for his friends to be brought to us by another way so that Maine would not see them. Two young men and a young woman were presented to us. They had heard about the old man claiming to be their friend. We asked them about the boy Maine and what they had done together growing up. The stories matched.

When asked if they would recognize Maine, they agreed that they would know him no matter what he had been through.

We had Maine brought in. He was profoundly ashamed of what he had done and become. It was difficult for him to raise his head and meet the eyes of his three friends. When he did the friends looked at him and were grieved to see what had become of their old friend.

They went to him one by one and we allowed it. The reunion was awkward at first, but his friends were true. They offered their comfort and help until he was better and could rebuild his life.

Life was good.

***

Two months passed and our men returned to us. Eli reported that they had found three portals and each and been destroyed. In the course of the mission they were able to save many lost souls, but many more were forever lost to us and they had to be killed. The weight of that was evident in the faces of every man. No mortal men were lost, though they carried deep wounds, both physical and emotional. They had proven to be excellent fighters. The men were rewarded with the last of the gold from King Harald's cache. Those from Breen were promoted to be our personal guard.

Random reports of people returning from Devil's possession continued to come to us from all parts of the world but no others returned to Breen. Eli felt compelled to travel and see to the spiritual needs of those people. He would record it all and on his return he would take his place as our historian. We agreed to let him go. Pinkert had history well in hand. Eli's history would compliment that nicely.

Life in Breen returned to normal and we prospered from the treaty and the fresh outlook of our citizens.

Otta gave birth to a healthy baby girl. Nine months later, we experienced another great miracle and I gave birth to a pink skinned baby girl with cinnamon colored hair. We named her Fionaghal. She was our greatest prize.

Fini

About the Author

Nance Bulow Morgan has been a photojournalist and worked in the print industry for three decades. A native of Northern Illinois, Bulow Morgan now resides in the Sandhills of North Carolina.

She has published a book of prose and a fantasy novel, Legend Destiny, that has become the spring board for a series titled The Minstrels' Tale Mystery. Minstrels' Gambit is the first in that series, followed by Minstrel's Covenant, and now Minstrels' Prize!

She is currently working on two projects, **Lionardo's Stone** (a fantasy roughly based on her favorite real life character; Lionardo DaVinci), and **A View From Here** (a compilation of her short stories).

Other Books by Nance Bulow-Morgan
Legend Destiny
Voyage: A Book of Prose
The Minstrels' Tale Mystery series:
- Minstrels' Gambit
- Minstrels' Covenant

Current Projects
Lionardo's Stone
A View From Here